The Crypt of

Where Truths Lie Buried

Max Donovan

Copyright © 2024 by Max Donovan

All rights reserved. No part of this book may be used or reproduced in any form whatsoever without written permission except in the case of brief quotations in critical articles or reviews.

First Edition: November 2024

Table of Contents

Chapter 1 The Councilman's Secret 1

Chapter 2 Symbols in the Shadows 19

Chapter 3 The Tunnels Beneath 36

Chapter 4 The Trap Unfolds 54

Chapter 5 Threats from the Dark 73

Chapter 6 Echoes of Betrayal 90

Chapter 7 Fragments of the Past 106

Chapter 8 The Order's Web 124

Chapter 9 The Legacy Revealed 138

Chapter 10 The Councilman's Motive 154

Chapter 11 A Mother's Warning 172

Chapter 12 Into the Depths 187

Chapter 13 The Core of the Conspiracy 203

Chapter 14 Unveiling the Experiment 220

Chapter 15 The Final Move 236

Epilogue The Shadows Endure 250

Chapter 1
The Councilman's Secret

The fluorescent lights in the councilman's office flickered, casting uneven shadows across the expansive room. Dr. Eliza Kain adjusted her gloves as she stepped carefully past the bodyguards stationed at the door. The marble floors amplified every sound, and the faint hum of her portable chemical analyzer punctuated the silence like a quiet metronome.

"Dr. Kain, thanks for getting here so quickly," the officer at the door said, his voice strained. "We've tried to secure the area, but—"

"Stop," Eliza said brusquely, holding up a gloved hand without breaking stride. "Anything you tell me might bias my analysis. Keep everyone out until I say otherwise." Her sharp blue eyes scanned the scene, taking in the scattered papers, the overturned chair, and, at the center, the lifeless body of Councilman Thomas Everard.

He was sprawled awkwardly across the marble, his face slack, eyes glassy, staring at the ceiling. A faint metallic object glinted in his outstretched hand—a key. Eliza crouched next to the body, her movements measured, and carefully adjusted her flashlight. The scene was meticulously arranged, too clean for a natural struggle. Every detail screamed orchestration.

"Councilman Everard," she murmured, tilting her head as her gloved hand hovered over his. "You didn't die of natural causes, did you?"

Her analyzer beeped softly, indicating faint traces of residue along the councilman's fingertips. She leaned in, her flashlight catching the bluish shimmer on his hand. The residue glowed faintly under the UV light. Synthetic. Unusual.

"Interesting," she whispered, tapping her earpiece. "Analyzer, scan composition."

A soft hum followed as her equipment began processing the sample. She let her gaze drift to the peculiar object in his hand—the key. It was heavier than it looked, its metallic surface engraved with intricate symbols. Carefully, she extracted it with her tweezers, inspecting it under the flashlight. Her breath hitched slightly, though her expression remained neutral.

"Not here," she murmured under her breath.

"Eliza," a voice called sharply from the doorway. Detective Marcus Hale stepped into the room, his broad shoulders and permanent scowl filling the doorway. "I see you've started without me. Again."

"Marcus," she replied evenly without looking up. "You're late. Again."

"Traffic," he quipped, his tone dry. He stepped closer, his boots echoing against the marble. "So, what are we looking at?"

"Quiet," she said sharply, holding the key closer to the light. "I'm not ready to brief you yet."

Marcus folded his arms, watching her with barely concealed irritation. "Let me guess. Fancy tech, synthetic compounds, and a murder mystery written all over it?"

Eliza sighed, straightening up. "If you must know, there's an unusual residue on his hand. Not industrial. And definitely not something you'd pick up casually."

She moved to the desk, her flashlight grazing its surface. Beneath the edge of the councilman's arm, faint etchings became visible—symbols carved into the polished wood. Eliza paused, her heartbeat quickening as she crouched down to examine them more closely.

"What now?" Marcus asked, peering over her shoulder. "More clues for your sci-fi journal?"

"Quiet," she snapped. Her finger traced one of the etchings, its precise angles and curves unsettlingly familiar. A flicker of memory surfaced—her mother's journal, filled with sketches of similar symbols. She blinked, pushing the thought aside.

"Eliza," Marcus said, his tone softening. "Talk to me. What are you seeing?"

"These symbols," she began slowly, standing up and stepping back from the desk. "They're not scratches from a struggle. They're deliberate. Someone carved them with intent."

"Intent," Marcus repeated, frowning. "Like a message?"

"Maybe," Eliza replied, though she avoided meeting his gaze. "Or a warning."

He folded his arms, his gaze shifting between her and the body. "You're thinking occult? Ritualistic? Don't say aliens."

She shot him a glare. "I don't jump to conclusions, unlike some people. But whatever it is, it's not random. Whoever did this wanted these symbols to be seen."

Marcus tilted his head, eyeing the symbols. "Seen by who? Us? Or you?"

The question lingered in the air for a moment. Eliza didn't answer. She returned her attention to the key, its weight unnervingly heavy in her gloved hand. It wasn't just a prop, she was certain—it was central to whatever had happened here.

"This key," she said after a long silence. "It's not just evidence. It's part of the reason he was killed."

Marcus arched a brow. "And you're sure about that?"

"Reasonably," she replied, pocketing the key and tapping her earpiece again. "Analyzer, status?"

"Scan complete," a robotic voice replied. "Unknown synthetic compound. Unregistered in public or industrial databases."

Marcus let out a low whistle. "That's a new one. You think this guy was messing with something experimental?"

"Or someone was messing with him," Eliza countered, her gaze drifting back to the desk.

The room felt colder suddenly, as if the symbols themselves carried a weight beyond the visible. Eliza straightened, brushing past Marcus toward the door. "We're taking this back to the lab. I need more data before I can say anything definitive."

"And the symbols?" he asked, following her.

Eliza paused, glancing over her shoulder. "They mean something. But until I know what, I'm keeping this to myself."

Marcus smirked faintly. "Of course you are. That's what you do."

The two of them stepped out, leaving the flickering lights to cast their jagged shadows over the lifeless councilman and the secrets etched into the desk.

The stillness of the office was broken by the steady rhythm of heavy footsteps approaching from the hallway. Detective Marcus Hale entered, his broad shoulders brushing against the doorframe as he took in the scene with a skeptical eye. His brown leather jacket was damp from the drizzle outside, and his dark eyes scanned the room with the practiced gaze of someone who'd seen far too many crime scenes.

"Eliza Kain, in the flesh," Marcus said, his voice cutting through the quiet hum of her equipment. His lips curled into the faintest smirk. "Always ahead of the curve, aren't you?"

Eliza didn't look up from the portable chemical analyzer in her hand, her gloved fingers tapping methodically on its touchscreen. "And you're always behind, Marcus," she replied, her tone neutral but pointed. "Traffic?"

"Call it detective's intuition. I figured I'd give you a head start," he shot back, crossing the room with a casual gait. His boots thudded against the marble floor as he stopped beside her, towering over her crouched frame. "What have we got?"

Eliza finally turned her gaze upward, meeting his with a look of mild annoyance. "You're standing in it."

Marcus's eyes shifted to the lifeless form of Councilman Everard sprawled on the floor. His brows furrowed as he took in the details—the peculiar angle of the body, the meticulously clean surroundings, the key still clutched in the councilman's hand. "Well, this is neat," he said dryly, crouching down beside her. "Too neat."

"Exactly," Eliza murmured, standing up and moving to the desk. Her flashlight traced faint lines etched into the polished wood. "This wasn't just a murder. It was arranged."

"Arranged how?" Marcus asked, his tone skeptical.

Eliza gestured toward the symbols carved into the desk. "Start with these. They're not accidental. Whoever did this wanted them noticed."

Marcus squinted at the markings, then snorted softly. "They look like doodles. Weird ones, sure, but… symbols?"

"Deliberate," Eliza corrected, her voice sharp. "Precise. And if you can't see the difference, maybe you need new glasses."

"Don't start," Marcus said, rising to his feet and brushing imaginary dust from his jacket. "What else?"

Eliza moved back to the councilman's body, pointing to the faint shimmer on his fingertips. "There's residue here. Synthetic. Unregistered in any public or industrial database."

Marcus raised an eyebrow. "Unregistered? You're saying someone cooked this up?"

"That's exactly what I'm saying," Eliza replied, her gaze steady. "This wasn't an accident or a random murder. It was planned, right down to the residue they left behind."

Marcus folded his arms, considering her words. "And the key? What's your take?"

"It's connected," Eliza said simply, pulling the metallic object from her evidence bag and holding it up to the light. The engraved symbols glinted faintly under the flickering fluorescent lights. "But I won't know how until I analyze it."

Marcus's skepticism was evident in his silence. He stepped closer to the desk, running a finger along the edge of one of the etched symbols. "You've got a theory, don't you?"

"I always have theories," Eliza said, her tone guarded. "But theories need evidence, and right now, I don't have enough to connect all the dots."

Marcus turned to her, a small grin tugging at the corner of his mouth. "And here I thought you liked jumping to conclusions."

Eliza shot him a sharp look. "I prefer following the evidence. You should try it sometime."

The banter hung in the air for a moment before Marcus sighed, his expression softening. "Look, I know you've got your fancy gadgets and your genius brain working overtime, but this? This looks like someone went to a lot of trouble to confuse us. Maybe we focus on the basics before diving into your sci-fi theories."

Eliza's jaw tightened. "And what would the basics tell us, Marcus? That a councilman is dead in his own office, holding a key to God-knows-what, with chemical residue on his hands that doesn't belong anywhere? If that's your version of basics, I'll pass."

Marcus chuckled softly, stepping back and raising his hands in mock surrender. "Fine. Do it your way. Just don't forget the part where we're supposed to build a case, not a conspiracy board."

Eliza turned away from him, her gaze fixed on the body once more. "A case won't mean much if we don't figure out what they're trying to hide."

For a moment, the room was silent except for the soft hum of the analyzer. Marcus leaned against the edge of the desk, watching her work with a mix of curiosity and grudging respect. He knew better than to push too hard when Eliza was in this state—focused, determined, and stubborn as hell.

"Anything else I should know?" he asked, his tone light but edged with sincerity.

Eliza didn't look up. "You'll know when I do."

Marcus sighed, shaking his head. "You really know how to keep a guy on his toes, Kain."

She allowed herself the faintest smile, though it was gone as quickly as it appeared. "Someone has to."

As Marcus straightened and took another glance around the room, Eliza's mind raced through the possibilities. The symbols, the residue, the key—they were pieces of a puzzle she didn't fully understand yet. But one thing was certain: whatever they were dealing with, it was far from ordinary.

And Eliza Kain didn't do ordinary.

Eliza held the key in her gloved hand, the metallic weight pressing against her palm. Its intricate symbols caught the light from her flashlight, the etchings sharp and deliberate. She ran her fingers across the grooves, her brow furrowing as a familiar unease crept into her chest.

"Okay, out with it," Marcus said, breaking the silence. He leaned against the desk, his arms crossed. "You've got that look again."

"What look?" she replied without glancing up.

"The one where you're halfway down a rabbit hole and already dragging me in after you."

She tilted the key slightly, studying the patterns. "These symbols," she began, her voice quiet but resolute, "they're not random. They're… deliberate."

"Deliberate," Marcus echoed, his tone laced with skepticism. "You've said that already. Elaborate."

"They're precise, mathematical," Eliza continued, ignoring his tone. "The angles, the spacing—it's like they were made to mean something specific."

"Yeah, well, anything carved with a steady hand can look deliberate," Marcus quipped. "Maybe the guy was just doodling. Stress relief gone wrong."

"On his desk? While clutching a key with matching symbols? Doesn't that seem a little too convenient?" She glanced at him briefly, her blue eyes sharp.

Marcus raised an eyebrow, his lips curling into a faint smirk. "Convenient, sure. But that's the kind of thing you forensic types love to overanalyze."

Eliza's fingers tightened around the key. "This isn't overanalysis, Marcus. I've seen these patterns before."

"Where? In one of your fancy textbooks?" He gestured vaguely to the analyzer and her equipment. "Or maybe in one of those sci-fi shows you pretend not to watch?"

She hesitated, her jaw tightening. "In my mother's notes."

That caught his attention. Marcus straightened slightly, his smirk fading. "Your mother? The historian?"

"The symbologist," Eliza corrected sharply. "She documented patterns like these in her research—patterns linked to ancient codes, secret organizations. Things most people dismissed as folklore."

"And now you're telling me it's not folklore?" Marcus's skepticism deepened. "Eliza, come on. You're connecting dots that aren't even in the same picture."

"You're not listening," she snapped, stepping closer to the desk. "These symbols aren't just meaningless scratches. They're part of something bigger. Something intentional."

"Something occult?" Marcus ventured, his voice dripping with sarcasm. "Because that's where this is headed, isn't it?"

"Possibly," she admitted, her voice steady. "Or something meant to appear occult, to send a message."

Marcus pinched the bridge of his nose, letting out a sigh. "Okay, let's say you're right and these symbols are part of some grand conspiracy. What does that have to do with a dead councilman?"

"That's what I intend to find out," Eliza replied, her grip on the key tightening. She looked at him, her expression firm. "But if I'm right, this wasn't just about him. It's bigger than one person."

Marcus barked a short laugh, shaking his head. "You really think someone offed a politician to… what? Write secret messages on a desk and leave you a puzzle to solve?"

"It's not about me," Eliza shot back, though a flicker of doubt crossed her face. "At least, I don't think it is. But whoever did this wanted someone to notice. Someone who could understand."

"Someone like you," Marcus said, pointing a finger at her. "Because let's be honest, Eliza, no one else is going to look at this and say, 'Oh, yeah, secret society for sure.'"

She didn't respond immediately, her eyes returning to the key. Its weight felt heavier now, as though the symbols themselves carried the gravity of what she was beginning to suspect.

"Marcus," she said finally, her tone softer but no less resolute, "I need to follow this lead."

"Of course you do," he muttered, throwing his hands up. "Because why not chase the wild theory instead of sticking to the basics?"

"This isn't just a theory," Eliza said, stepping closer. "You know me. I don't waste time on dead ends."

"No," he admitted grudgingly. "You just drag me into them."

Her lips twitched into the faintest hint of a smile. "Then consider this your lucky day. Because this isn't a dead end. It's the start of something much bigger."

Marcus studied her for a long moment, his expression unreadable. Finally, he let out a resigned sigh. "Fine. But if this turns into some Da Vinci Code nonsense, I'm blaming you."

"Noted," she replied, slipping the key into her evidence bag. "Now, let's get back to the lab. I need to see what this residue is and how it connects."

Marcus gestured toward the body as they started for the door. "And what about him?"

"We document everything, as usual," Eliza said, not breaking stride. "But the key and the symbols are what matter now. They'll lead us to the truth."

"And if they don't?" he asked, a note of challenge in his voice.

"They will," she replied without hesitation, the weight of her certainty matching the weight of the key in her hand.

The councilman's office was still as Eliza turned off her flashlight and switched to the UV light attachment on her portable scanner. The room bathed in an ethereal blue glow, revealing stains, fingerprints, and smudges invisible to the naked eye. As she swept the light across the polished desk, something caught her attention—faint streaks running parallel to the carved symbols.

"Eliza," Marcus said from the corner of the room, his voice cautious. "You're scanning a desk like it's going to confess. What are you hoping to find?"

"Answers," she replied curtly, focusing the beam on the markings. "Look at this."

Marcus approached, his hands in his jacket pockets as he peered over her shoulder. "What am I supposed to be looking at?"

"These," Eliza said, pointing to the faint markings that crisscrossed the surface. "They're invisible without UV light. Whoever carved the symbols tried to clean up afterward, but they left traces."

"Traces of what?" Marcus leaned closer, squinting. "More symbols?"

"No," she said, angling the light. "These are different. They're… directional."

"Directional?" he repeated, his brow furrowing. "Like pointing to something?"

"Possibly," Eliza said. Her voice was calm, but her mind was racing. The additional markings didn't match the precision of the carved symbols, but they were deliberate. They were leading somewhere. "I need to analyze this further. It could be nothing, or it could be—"

"A breadcrumb trail," Marcus finished, standing upright. "You're thinking someone left this here on purpose."

"It's likely," she admitted. "Everything about this scene feels intentional. If they wanted us to find the key, the symbols, and now these markings…"

"Then they're playing games," Marcus interjected. He crossed his arms, his voice laced with irritation. "And I hate games."

Eliza smirked faintly, still focused on her scan. "Good thing I'm here then. I like games."

Marcus rolled his eyes, but there was no hiding his curiosity as he continued to watch her work. "You seriously think these faint lines mean something? Couldn't it just be scratches from… I don't know, an angry janitor?"

"Unlikely," she replied. "The directionality is too specific. See how they converge here?" She pointed to the edge of the desk, where the faint lines gathered like tributaries meeting a river. "They're pointing to something."

Marcus exhaled sharply, pinching the bridge of his nose. "You know, I had plans tonight. Something simple, quiet. Maybe a burger. And now I'm here, looking at glowy scratch marks."

"Welcome to my world," Eliza said absently, moving to the councilman's hand again. She used the UV light to scan his fingertips, where the residue still clung. The bluish shimmer revealed something new—smaller symbols, faintly imprinted on his skin.

Her breath hitched. "Marcus, look at this."

"What now?" he asked, stepping closer. His eyes widened as he saw the tiny, intricate designs glowing under the UV light. "What is that? A tattoo?"

"No," Eliza said, shaking her head. "It's residue from the key."

Marcus raised an eyebrow. "You're telling me the key left a pattern on his fingers?"

"That's exactly what I'm telling you," she said, her voice tight. "Whoever made this key didn't just engrave it for aesthetics. It's designed to transfer these symbols—like a stamp."

"A stamp for what?" Marcus's skepticism was evident. "This isn't making sense, Eliza."

"It's not supposed to," she replied, slipping the key back into her evidence bag. "At least, not yet. But this just became a lot more complicated."

Marcus let out a low whistle, stepping back and running a hand through his hair. "All right, fine. Take it to the lab. Run your tests, do your thing. But don't forget we still have a dead councilman and a case to build."

"I haven't forgotten," Eliza said firmly, standing up and packing her equipment. "The lab results will tell us what we need to know. This residue, these symbols—they're the key to understanding why he was killed."

Marcus's smirk returned. "Pun intended?"

"Completely accidental," she said with a faint smile, heading toward the door. "I'll call you once I've got something solid."

"Don't keep me waiting too long," Marcus called after her. "I don't want to hear about this from your lab rats before I hear it from you."

Eliza didn't respond as she left the office, the evidence bag slung over her shoulder and her thoughts racing. The key felt heavier in her mind than it had in her hand. The intricate symbols, the faint residue, the convergence of markings—it all pointed to something much larger than a simple murder.

Later, alone in the quiet of her car, she pulled out her mother's journal. The leather cover was worn from years of handling, and the familiar smell of old paper wafted up as she opened it.

Her fingers flipped to a page filled with sketches of symbols, notes scrawled in her mother's precise handwriting.

There it was—the same pattern. Her mother had seen it before. Documented it. But why? And how was it connected to the councilman's death?

Eliza stared at the page, her thumb brushing against the faded ink. The symbols weren't just part of the case. They were part of her past, of her mother's unfinished work. And now, they had become her responsibility.

She closed the journal, her resolve hardening. Whatever this was, she wasn't going to let it slip into the shadows. Not again.

Chapter 2
Symbols in the Shadows

The quiet hum of the apartment seemed louder than usual as Eliza dropped her evidence bag on the counter and shrugged off her coat. She made a beeline for the bookshelf tucked into the corner of the room, her fingers trailing over the spines of well-worn books until she found the one she was looking for.

The leather-bound journal was unassuming, its cover scuffed from years of handling. Eliza hesitated for a moment before pulling it free. She carried it to her desk, the weight of it heavier in her hands than it had ever been before.

"Mom," she murmured under her breath, flipping open the cover to reveal the familiar, precise handwriting on the first page. "What were you trying to tell me?"

The pages whispered as she turned them, her fingers brushing over old ink and faded diagrams. She stopped when she saw it—a page filled with intricate symbols that mirrored the ones she had seen etched into the councilman's desk. Her breath caught in her throat.

"You've got to be kidding me," she whispered.

Her mother's handwriting wrapped around the sketches like ivy, the words meticulous and deliberate: *'Binding truths in plain sight. Guarded by those who would wield them.'*

"What does that even mean?" Eliza muttered, leaning closer to study the symbols. They were identical, down to the precise angles and curves. It wasn't a coincidence. It couldn't be.

Her mind drifted back to her mother's warnings, cryptic words spoken in the soft light of their living room so many years ago. The memory unfolded like a film reel, vivid and unyielding.

"Eliza, listen to me," her mother's voice echoed in her mind, calm but insistent. "Symbols like these aren't just decorations. They're codes, messages hidden in plain sight."

"Codes for what?" Eliza, no older than sixteen, had asked, her arms crossed over her chest. She'd thought it was another one of her mother's academic tangents, fascinating but irrelevant to their daily lives.

"For understanding," her mother had replied, tapping the edge of the journal with her pen. "And for power. People who know how to read them can find the truth—or hide it."

Eliza had scoffed, rolling her eyes. "You make it sound like a spy movie."

Her mother's expression had softened, but her tone remained serious. "It's not fiction, Eliza. These symbols have been used for centuries, and not always by people with good intentions."

"Like who?" Eliza had challenged, leaning forward. "Secret societies? The Illuminati?"

Her mother's lips had pressed into a thin line. "Don't mock what you don't understand. One day, you might wish you'd listened."

The memory faded, and Eliza found herself gripping the edges of the journal, her knuckles white. She hadn't taken her mother seriously back then, brushing off her warnings as eccentricities of a brilliant but overly imaginative mind. But now? Now she wasn't so sure.

She tapped her fingers against the desk, her eyes scanning the sketches and notes. The symbols on the councilman's desk weren't just eerily similar—they were the same. Her mother had known about them, studied them, and yet she had never explained why they mattered.

Eliza's thoughts were interrupted by the ringing of her phone. She glanced at the screen—Marcus.

"Perfect timing," she muttered, picking up the call. "What is it, Marcus?"

"What's it ever?" his voice came through, gruff but tinged with humor. "You disappear without a word, and I'm left to deal with the fallout. I figured I'd check if you've solved the whole thing yet."

"I'm working on it," she replied, her tone clipped as she leaned back in her chair. "I found something."

"Of course, you did," he said, a note of sarcasm in his voice. "Go on, hit me with it. Symbols, magic keys, hidden treasure?"

"Not far off," she said, ignoring his tone. "The symbols we found at the scene—they're identical to ones my mother documented in her research."

There was a pause on the other end of the line. "Your mother? You're dragging family into this now?"

"She was a symbologist, Marcus," Eliza snapped. "She spent her life studying patterns like these, and now they're showing up in a murder investigation."

"You're serious," he said, his skepticism giving way to genuine curiosity. "All right, what did she say about them?"

"Not enough," Eliza admitted, glancing back at the journal. "But what she did say was clear—they're not meaningless. They're messages, or warnings, or… something."

Marcus let out a low whistle. "Well, that's comforting. So, what's your next move?"

"I analyze the residue," she said firmly. "If my mother was right, and these symbols mean something, then whoever killed the councilman didn't leave them there by accident."

"And if she was wrong?" Marcus asked, his voice softer now. "What if this is just another dead end?"

Eliza's grip on the journal tightened. "She wasn't wrong," she said quietly. "I'll prove it."

For a moment, there was only silence between them. Then Marcus cleared his throat. "All right, Kain. I'll back you on this, but you'd better find something concrete. No pressure."

"None taken," she said, ending the call. She placed the phone beside the journal and leaned back in her chair, her mind a swirl of questions and half-formed theories.

The symbols stared back at her from the page, as enigmatic and infuriating as ever. Her mother had believed in their importance, and now, decades later, they were demanding her attention once again. But this time, Eliza wouldn't ignore them. She couldn't.

The sharp scent of disinfectant hung in the air as Marcus stepped into Eliza's lab, his footsteps heavy against the polished tile floor. His eyes immediately darted around the space, taking in the organized chaos of monitors, chemical analyzers, and evidence bags scattered across the countertops. He found her at the center of it all, hunched over a glowing screen, her face illuminated by its pale light.

"Eliza," he called, his tone cutting through the low hum of the equipment.

She didn't look up. "Not now, Marcus."

"Yeah, yeah, I know," he said, stepping closer. "You're busy cracking the case wide open. But here's the thing—you left me hanging. Again."

She sighed, straightening up and turning to face him. "What do you want, Marcus?"

"An update," he said, gesturing broadly to the lab. "Preferably one that doesn't involve glowing symbols or ancient conspiracies."

She crossed her arms, leaning back against the counter. "The residue from the councilman's hand is synthetic, as I suspected. Unregistered. Someone went to a lot of trouble to make sure it couldn't be traced."

"And the key?" Marcus asked, his eyes narrowing.

"Same story," Eliza replied. "The material isn't anything special, but the engravings... they're another matter."

Marcus arched a brow. "Here we go. Let me guess—more symbols of doom and gloom?"

She ignored his sarcasm. "They're precise, mathematical. They match the ones on the councilman's desk and... other sources."

"Other sources?" He tilted his head, catching the hesitation in her voice. "What aren't you telling me?"

"Nothing relevant," she said quickly, turning back to the screen. "The evidence speaks for itself."

Marcus stepped closer, his gaze sharp as it landed on the leather-bound journal sitting beside her keyboard. He reached for it, flipping it open before she could stop him. His eyes scanned the pages, his frown deepening. "This your mom's?"

Eliza froze for a moment before snatching the journal from his hands. "That's personal."

"Personal?" he repeated, incredulous. "Eliza, this is a murder investigation, and you've got a symbology journal sitting next to forensic evidence. You don't see the problem here?"

"There is no problem," she snapped, slamming the journal shut. "My mother's research is relevant, that's all."

"Relevant how?" Marcus pressed. "You're not exactly being transparent here."

She hesitated, her fingers tightening around the journal. "She documented similar symbols in her work. That's it."

Marcus crossed his arms, his expression skeptical. "That's it? Come on, Eliza. You're not just using her research—you're chasing her ghost. You can't let that cloud your judgment."

"It's not clouding anything," she said, her voice cold. "The evidence will prove what's real and what's not."

He leaned against the counter, his gaze unwavering. "Will it? Because right now, it looks like you're letting this get personal."

She turned away from him, placing the journal carefully on a nearby shelf. "This isn't about me, Marcus. It's about the councilman, the symbols, and whoever orchestrated this."

"But it is about you," he said, stepping closer. "You wouldn't be this invested if it weren't."

Eliza spun back around, her eyes flashing. "You don't know what you're talking about."

"Don't I?" Marcus shot back. "You've been off your game ever since we found those symbols. You're holding something back, Eliza, and if you don't trust me enough to share it, then what the hell are we doing here?"

For a moment, the room was silent except for the soft hum of the equipment. Eliza stared at him, her jaw tight. Finally, she let out a slow breath, her shoulders relaxing slightly.

"Fine," she said quietly. "Yes, this is personal. But that doesn't mean I'm wrong."

Marcus softened, but only slightly. "Look, I'm not saying you're wrong. I'm saying you need to separate the personal from the professional. Otherwise, you're just handing the other side an advantage."

She nodded, her gaze dropping to the floor. "I know."

He studied her for a moment before stepping back, his tone gentler. "So, what's the next step?"

She straightened, her professional mask slipping back into place. "The lab results will give us more to work with. Until then, I'll keep analyzing the symbols and comparing them to what we've found at the scene."

"And the journal?" Marcus asked, glancing at the shelf where she'd placed it.

"It stays here," she said firmly. "I won't let it interfere."

Marcus nodded, though his expression remained cautious. "All right. But if you start seeing ghosts, I'm calling you out."

"Duly noted," she said, a faint smile tugging at her lips.

He returned the smile, albeit faintly, and pushed off the counter. "Just don't forget to let me know when you actually find something concrete. I'm not exactly a fan of sitting on my hands."

"I'll keep you updated," she promised, turning back to her workstation.

As Marcus left the lab, the tension lingered in the air. Eliza glanced at the journal on the shelf, her mind racing with half-formed theories and unanswered questions. Personal or not, she couldn't ignore the connection between her mother's work and the case. But for now, she'd keep that to herself.

Eliza sat at her workstation, the journal open beside her as the hum of her lab equipment filled the air. Her eyes flitted between the screen displaying the results of the residue analysis and the faded sketches in her mother's journal. Each piece of data seemed to add weight to the growing puzzle, but none of it offered a clear solution.

"Come on," she muttered under her breath, tapping her fingers against the desk. "Give me something solid."

The analyzer beeped, its digital readout updating with the final analysis. Eliza leaned forward, her brow furrowing as she scanned the results. Synthetic. Unregistered. A complex compound that didn't match anything in public or industrial databases.

She leaned back in her chair, exhaling slowly. "Custom-made. Just like I thought."

Her gaze shifted to the journal, where her mother's handwriting curled around a detailed sketch of a symbol eerily similar to the ones found at the crime scene. As she flipped through the pages, a loose photograph slipped out and fluttered onto the desk.

"What's this?" Eliza murmured, picking it up.

The photograph was old, the edges worn and slightly yellowed. It showed a group of people standing on the steps of a government building, their faces serious and their postures rigid. At the center of the group stood her mother, younger but unmistakably confident, her expression calm and composed.

Eliza's stomach tightened. Her mother had rarely mentioned her fieldwork outside academia, and she'd never spoken about anything involving government buildings or groups like this.

Her fingers brushed the corner of the photo, her eyes scanning the background. The building looked familiar, its imposing columns and intricate facade hinting at significance. Then it clicked—the building wasn't just any government site. It had a reputation, whispered about in obscure corners of academic circles. Rumored to house secretive organizations. Rumored to have ties to the Concordant Order.

Eliza stared at the photograph, her pulse quickening. "Mom," she whispered, her voice tinged with disbelief. "What were you doing there?"

Before she could lose herself in speculation, the door to her lab swung open, and Marcus strode in. His expression was a mix of curiosity and impatience.

"Don't you ever lock your doors?" Eliza asked, tucking the photograph into the journal as he approached.

"Don't you ever answer your phone?" Marcus shot back, gesturing to the silent device sitting on her desk. "I've been trying to get ahold of you for an hour."

"Busy," she said shortly, gesturing to the screen. "The residue's synthetic. Completely unregistered. Whoever made it wanted to stay off the radar."

Marcus peered at the readout, his brow furrowing. "So, what does that mean? Black market chemicals? Some secret government lab?"

"Possibly," she said, her tone measured. "But look at this." She pulled up a digital rendering of the residue's molecular structure. "It's complex, more than anything you'd find in standard industrial use. This wasn't made for mass production. It was designed for something specific."

"Specific like what?" Marcus asked, his skepticism evident.

"That's what I'm trying to figure out," Eliza replied. She hesitated for a moment, then opened the journal to the page with the symbols. "These symbols—they're connected somehow."

Marcus groaned, dragging a hand down his face. "Not this again."

"Just listen," Eliza said sharply. She pointed to the photograph tucked into the journal. "This fell out while I was working."

Marcus leaned in, his eyes narrowing as he studied the image. "Is that… your mom?"

"Yes," Eliza said, her voice tight. "And that building? It's rumored to have ties to the Concordant Order."

"The what?" Marcus asked, looking genuinely baffled.

"The Concordant Order," she repeated, her tone clipped. "A secretive organization tied to symbols like these. My mother studied them."

"And you think they're connected to the councilman's death?" Marcus asked, his tone skeptical but no longer dismissive.

"I don't think—it's more than that," Eliza replied. "This isn't just academic theory, Marcus. These symbols, the residue, the key—they're all part of something deliberate."

Marcus exhaled sharply, running a hand through his hair. "Okay, let's say you're right. What does that mean for us? Are we chasing down secret societies now?"

Eliza shook her head. "We're following the evidence. And right now, the evidence is pointing to the Concordant Order."

Marcus was silent for a moment, his gaze flicking between her and the journal. Finally, he nodded, though his expression remained wary. "Fine. But you'd better have more than a photograph and some glowing chemicals if you expect me to put this in the report."

Eliza managed a faint smile. "Give me time. The truth will come out."

"It always does," Marcus muttered, pushing off the counter. "Just make sure you don't go too deep down this rabbit hole without me."

As he left, Eliza turned back to the photograph. Her fingers traced the edge of the image, her mind racing with questions. What had her mother been involved in? And how deep did this connection to the Concordant Order go?

The pieces were there, scattered like fragments of a shattered mirror. Now she just had to find a way to put them together.

Eliza stared at the molecular structure on her computer screen, the complex lattice glowing faintly against the dark interface. The residue's synthetic makeup was intricate, almost elegant in its precision. It wasn't just unregistered; it was engineered with a level of expertise that screamed exclusivity.

She typed a series of commands into the system, cross-referencing the compound against private databases she had access to through old academic channels. The screen populated with a series of names—labs, suppliers, research facilities. Most were legitimate, their records clean. But one name at the bottom of the list made her pause.

"Caliber Chemical Industries," she murmured aloud. The name was familiar, and not in a reassuring way.

The sound of the lab door opening startled her. Marcus stepped in again, his usual mix of curiosity and skepticism plastered on his face. "Back so soon?" she asked, glancing at him.

"Still no locks on your doors," he quipped, leaning against the counter. "Thought I'd check in before you disappeared down another rabbit hole."

"Good timing," she said, gesturing to the screen. "I found something."

Marcus approached, his gaze narrowing as he read the highlighted name. "Caliber Chemical Industries. Should I be impressed?"

"You should be concerned," Eliza said, her voice tight. "This supplier isn't just a chemical manufacturer. They've been flagged in multiple investigations for off-the-books projects and untraceable compounds."

Marcus let out a low whistle. "And you think they made this residue?"

"I'd bet on it," she replied, crossing her arms. "Their methods match. Everything they produce is custom, and they cater to clients who want discretion above all else."

"And let me guess," Marcus said, his tone dripping with sarcasm, "you think they're tied to your secret society—the Concordant Order?"

"I don't think," she said firmly. "I know. Look at this." She pulled up another window, displaying financial records she'd accessed through back channels. "Caliber's biggest client is a shell company. Its only documented activity? Massive deposits and purchases tied to properties linked to Order rumors."

"Rumors," Marcus repeated, arching a brow. "Not exactly solid evidence."

"It's a pattern," Eliza countered. "One that keeps leading back to the same place."

Marcus rubbed the back of his neck, glancing between her and the screen. "Okay, say you're right. What do we do with this? You can't exactly kick down the doors of a chemical supplier and demand answers."

"I wasn't planning on kicking down doors," she said, her tone sharp. "But I can look into their supply chain. Find out who's buying what and where it's going."

"And how exactly do you plan to do that?" Marcus asked. "You think they're just going to hand over their client list because you asked nicely?"

"Of course not," Eliza said, a small smirk tugging at her lips. "That's why I have you."

"Me?" Marcus looked genuinely startled. "What am I supposed to do? Flash my badge and hope they're feeling cooperative?"

"You're a detective," she said simply. "You know how to ask questions without raising alarms. Start with the surface-level inquiries—who runs their day-to-day operations, what kind of clients they typically handle. That'll give me enough to dig deeper."

"And what will you be doing while I'm playing nice?" Marcus asked, folding his arms.

"Tracking down their most recent shipments," she replied, her focus shifting back to the screen. "If we can figure out where this residue was delivered, we'll have a lead."

Marcus sighed, running a hand through his hair. "You really don't make this easy, do you?"

"Would you still be here if I did?" she shot back, glancing at him with a faint smile.

He chuckled despite himself. "Fair point. Fine, I'll see what I can dig up. But if this goes sideways, you owe me dinner."

"Deal," she said, her tone light but determined.

As Marcus left the lab, Eliza turned back to her workstation. The name Caliber Chemical Industries lingered on the screen, a glaring reminder of the web she was unraveling. Her fingers hovered over the keyboard for a moment before she opened another database, pulling up property records tied to the supplier.

The more she searched, the clearer the picture became. Caliber wasn't just a chemical supplier—they were a hub, a nexus for activity that didn't want to be traced. And the deeper she dug, the more the Concordant Order's influence loomed over every transaction and connection.

By the time she stepped away from her desk, her resolve was solidified. She grabbed her coat and slung it over her shoulders, her mind racing with possibilities. The supplier was her next move. If she could uncover their ties to the councilman's death, she'd finally have a lead strong enough to follow.

As she locked the lab and stepped out into the crisp night air, one thought repeated in her mind: *This isn't just a case anymore. It's a trail—and I'm going to follow it.*

Chapter 3
The Tunnels Beneath

The abandoned factory loomed before them, a hulking mass of rusted metal and shattered glass against the gray, overcast sky. Weeds sprouted through cracks in the pavement, and the faint smell of decay lingered in the air. Eliza stood at the entrance, adjusting her forensic glasses, the high-tech lenses scanning for any trace of the synthetic compound they had traced back to this site.

"Charming place," Marcus muttered as he stepped up beside her. His eyes darted around the empty yard, his hand instinctively brushing against the holster at his side. "This is exactly where I'd go if I wanted to disappear forever."

"It's not about disappearing," Eliza replied, her tone clipped as she activated the glasses. "It's about hiding something in plain sight."

The glasses emitted a soft chime as they began their analysis, scanning the ground and surrounding surfaces. Eliza took a cautious step forward, her boots crunching against the gravel. The faint blue overlay of the glasses highlighted traces of the chemical compound, glowing faintly against the worn concrete. The trail was faint but distinct, leading toward the factory's gaping entrance.

"Found something," she said, gesturing for Marcus to follow. "Traces of the residue. Whoever was here didn't do a perfect job of covering their tracks."

Marcus followed, his eyes darting toward the shadows cast by the building's towering walls. "Let's hope they're not still around."

Inside, the factory was a labyrinth of rusted machinery and forgotten debris. Shafts of light filtered through the broken windows, casting eerie patterns on the floor. Eliza scanned the area, the faint chemical trail winding through the cluttered space like a ghostly thread. Her glasses flagged faint fingerprints on a steel beam, and she paused to take a closer look.

"Deliberate," she murmured to herself, noting the precision of the smudges. They weren't the random marks of someone passing through—they were intentional, placed as though to guide someone deeper into the factory.

Marcus stood a few paces behind her, his hand now firmly on his holstered weapon. "What are you seeing?"

"Breadcrumbs," she replied, moving toward a rusted staircase. The chemical trail glowed faintly on the steps, leading upward to a shadowy mezzanine. "Whoever was here wanted to leave a trail. They weren't trying to hide."

"That's comforting," Marcus said dryly, glancing around the cavernous space. "So, what's the play? Follow the breadcrumbs and hope they don't lead us into a trap?"

Eliza paused at the base of the staircase, considering his words. "It's a risk," she admitted, "but we won't find answers by staying safe."

Marcus sighed, muttering under his breath. "I hate it when you're right."

As they ascended the creaking staircase, the chemical trail grew stronger, the glow more vibrant. Eliza adjusted her glasses, her gaze narrowing as the trail led them to a rusted hatch embedded in the mezzanine floor. It was partially hidden beneath a pile of discarded crates, but the faint shimmer of residue around its edges gave it away.

"There," she said, pointing to the hatch. "That's where the trail leads."

Marcus crouched beside the hatch, running his fingers along its edge. "Looks like it hasn't been opened in years."

"It has," Eliza countered, kneeling beside him. Her glasses highlighted faint scuff marks and scratches on the metal. "Recently, too. Someone's been using this."

Marcus shook his head, glancing around the mezzanine. "This whole setup feels wrong. It's too… deliberate."

"I know," Eliza said quietly. She reached into her bag and pulled out a small tool, working to loosen the hatch. "But we're here now. We have to see where this goes."

The hatch groaned as it swung open, revealing a narrow ladder descending into darkness. A faint chemical smell wafted up from below, the same synthetic tang as the residue they had been tracking.

Marcus peered into the darkness, his jaw tightening. "If you tell me we're going down there, I might actually quit."

"We're going down there," Eliza said without hesitation. She activated the light on her glasses, illuminating the ladder and the narrow passage below.

Marcus let out a low groan but stepped aside, gesturing for her to go first. "Fine. But if something jumps out at us, I'm shooting first and asking questions never."

Eliza smirked faintly, lowering herself onto the ladder. "Noted."

As she descended into the darkness, the chemical trail grew stronger, the faint glow of her glasses illuminating a narrow tunnel carved into the earth. The air was damp and heavy, carrying the faint echo of dripping water. Eliza reached the bottom and stepped aside to make room for Marcus, her heart pounding as she took in her surroundings.

The walls of the tunnel were lined with markings, symbols etched into the stone that sent a chill down her spine. They matched the ones from the councilman's office, their presence here both confirming her suspicions and deepening the mystery.

Marcus joined her, his flashlight cutting through the gloom. He froze as his beam landed on the symbols. "Well, that's not creepy at all."

Eliza's voice was steady, though her pulse raced. "We're close. Whoever left these symbols wants us to find something."

Marcus shook his head, his expression grim. "Or they want to make sure we don't leave."

The tunnel stretched ahead, dark and foreboding. Eliza tightened her grip on her bag, her resolve hardening. Whatever waited for them at the end of the trail, she knew one thing for certain—they couldn't turn back now.

The narrow tunnel opened into a larger underground chamber, the air thick and musty. The faint chemical trail that had guided Eliza and Marcus here dissipated into the stale atmosphere, leaving them standing in a room lined with rusted cabinets, broken shelving, and the remains of what might have once been an organized workspace.

Eliza adjusted her forensic glasses, scanning the walls for any residual traces. The faint blue glow highlighted scratches and markings etched into the stone, but nothing immediately useful. Her eyes narrowed as she stepped closer to one of the cabinets, the metallic surface corroded but intact.

"This place feels like a graveyard," Marcus muttered, his flashlight beam sweeping the room. "Or a trap."

"It's not a trap," Eliza said, her voice distracted as she examined the cabinet. "At least not yet."

"That's reassuring," Marcus replied dryly, his footsteps echoing as he moved cautiously toward the far side of the chamber. "So, what are we looking for? A big neon sign that says 'Conspiracy Headquarters'?"

"Something more subtle," Eliza countered, prying open the cabinet door. It groaned in protest, revealing a set of compartments sealed with rusted locks. Her gaze sharpened as she pulled out her multi-tool, working on the first lock with practiced precision. "These aren't random markings. They're precise. Deliberate."

Marcus leaned against the wall, watching her work. "You keep saying that. Deliberate how?"

"Whoever was here didn't want casual intruders finding this," she said, her focus on the lock. "They weren't hiding everything, but they weren't advertising either."

"And you're thinking the Concordant Order?" Marcus asked, his skepticism evident.

"I'm thinking whoever left those symbols wanted someone to find this eventually," Eliza replied, the lock finally giving way with a metallic snap. She opened the compartment, revealing a tightly rolled piece of parchment.

She unfolded it carefully, her glasses enhancing the faded ink that sprawled across the weathered material. It was a map—an intricate layout of the city's underground network, complete with detailed notations and markings.

"Bingo," Eliza murmured, spreading the map across the nearest surface.

Marcus stepped closer, his flashlight illuminating the map's details. "Okay, I'll bite. What am I looking at?"

"It's a schematic of the city's tunnels," Eliza said, her fingers tracing the lines. "Sewer systems, old train routes, forgotten utility pathways… and more."

"More?" Marcus asked, his brow furrowing.

"These markings," she said, pointing to several spots on the map where symbols similar to the ones they'd found earlier were etched. "They're not part of the original infrastructure. These were added later. Deliberately."

"There's that word again," Marcus muttered. He leaned in, squinting at the symbols. "Wait—this one here. Isn't that near the councilman's office?"

"It is," Eliza confirmed, her voice taut. "And this one," she pointed to another symbol, "lines up with the factory we just came from."

Marcus straightened, his expression darkening. "So, what are you saying? The tunnels are being used for… what? Smuggling? Secret meetings?"

"Covert operations," Eliza said, her tone measured. "The councilman might have stumbled onto this. Maybe he found out what the tunnels were being used for—or who was using them."

Marcus let out a low whistle, rubbing the back of his neck. "And you think the Order's behind it?"

"I don't think it's a coincidence," Eliza said, scanning the rest of the map. "The Order's influence has always been tied to secrecy and control. These tunnels give them both."

"And murder, apparently," Marcus added, his voice grim. "If the councilman was poking around this, it'd be a good reason to silence him."

Eliza nodded, her fingers lingering on the map. "We need to figure out what these marked sites mean. If the Order is using these tunnels, there's a reason."

Marcus gestured toward the map. "And you think we'll find answers by following this thing? Looks like a lot of dark corners to poke around in."

"It's all we've got," Eliza said simply. She rolled up the map and slid it into her bag, her expression resolute. "If we can figure out their operations, we'll get closer to understanding why the councilman was killed."

"Closer to danger, too," Marcus pointed out. "These people don't exactly strike me as the forgiving type."

"I'm not looking for forgiveness," Eliza replied, her tone cold. "I'm looking for the truth."

Marcus sighed, pushing off the wall. "Fine. But if we end up lost in some underground maze because of that thing, I'm blaming you."

"Noted," Eliza said with a faint smirk. She adjusted her glasses and scanned the room one last time, ensuring nothing was left behind.

The chamber felt heavier as they prepared to leave, the map now a tangible link to something much larger than either of them had anticipated. Eliza could feel the weight of it pressing down on her, the symbols and their meanings whispering promises of secrets yet to be uncovered.

As they climbed back into the tunnel, her grip tightened on her bag. Whatever waited at the end of this trail, she knew one thing for certain: they were no longer following breadcrumbs. They were walking straight into the heart of the mystery.

The tunnel grew narrower as Eliza and Marcus moved forward, their footsteps echoing faintly off the damp stone walls. The air was colder here, the faint chemical scent replaced by the earthy tang of mildew. Eliza's forensic glasses scanned ahead, casting a soft glow onto the walls, but her unease grew with every step. The shadows seemed to shift unnaturally, though she dismissed it as a trick of the dim light.

Marcus was less composed. He kept one hand hovering near his holster, his eyes darting between the walls and the floor. "I don't like this," he muttered, his voice low.

"You don't like anything," Eliza shot back, her tone sharper than she intended. "We're fine. The tunnel's clear."

"For now," Marcus replied, his voice tight. "But doesn't this place feel… off to you?"

"Off how?" she asked, her attention still focused on her glasses' scan.

"I don't know," he said, glancing over his shoulder. "Like we're being watched."

Before she could respond, a faint sound echoed through the tunnel—a soft scuff of movement, almost imperceptible. Eliza froze, her hand instinctively tightening around the strap of her bag. Marcus drew his weapon, the click of his holster breaking the tense silence.

"You heard that, right?" he whispered.

She nodded, her voice barely audible. "It could be anything. Rats, debris shifting…"

"Or someone who doesn't want us here," Marcus finished, his grip on the gun steady as his eyes scanned the darkness ahead. "Stay close."

They moved forward cautiously, the tunnel stretching into the shadows. The sound came again, this time closer—a faint shuffle, like someone shifting their weight. Eliza's heart raced, though she forced herself to stay focused. Her glasses highlighted faint fibers caught on a jagged edge of the wall, the threads fresh and out of place in the dusty environment.

"Look at this," she whispered, gesturing to the fibers. "Someone's been through here recently."

Marcus glanced at the threads, then back at the tunnel ahead. "Great. So we're not alone."

Eliza crouched, examining the fibers more closely. "These are synthetic. High-tensile, like from tactical gear. Whoever left them wasn't just passing through."

"Fantastic," Marcus said under his breath, his tone laced with sarcasm. "So now we're dealing with people who know how to gear up. Just keeps getting better."

Another sound—this time a faint clink of metal—echoed from somewhere deeper in the tunnel. Marcus spun toward the noise, his gun raised. "That wasn't a rat."

"No," Eliza agreed, standing quickly. "And it wasn't debris either."

Marcus motioned for her to stay behind him as they advanced. His flashlight beam cut through the darkness, revealing nothing but the rough stone walls and the faint footprints in the dirt—a trail leading further into the labyrinthine tunnels. The prints were fresh, the edges still crisp.

"They were just here," Marcus said, his voice barely above a whisper. "We're not chasing ghosts, Eliza. These people are real."

Eliza's throat tightened. "So where are they now?"

"That's the million-dollar question," he muttered, his eyes scanning the tunnel ahead. "And I'm guessing we won't like the answer."

The tension was suffocating as they continued. Every sound seemed amplified, every shadow a potential threat. The tunnel widened slightly, opening into a smaller chamber with an uneven floor. Marcus's flashlight swept the room, catching faint scuffs and disturbed dust near the far wall.

"They stopped here," he said, motioning toward the marks. "But why?"

Eliza's glasses picked up faint traces of the chemical residue again, leading toward a narrow gap in the wall. "They went through there," she said, pointing to the opening.

Marcus frowned. "That's barely wide enough for a person."

"Exactly," she said, her voice steady despite the knot in her stomach. "It's a bottleneck. If they're ahead, they'll know we're coming."

"Perfect," Marcus said dryly. He turned back to her, his expression serious. "We can't keep walking into this blind, Eliza. If they're watching us, they've got the upper hand."

"I know," she admitted, adjusting her glasses. "But if we stop now, we lose the trail."

Marcus sighed, his frustration evident. "You're not going to let this go, are you?"

She met his gaze, her resolve unwavering. "Not a chance."

He muttered something under his breath before turning back toward the gap. "Fine. But if this goes south, we're getting out. No arguments."

"Deal," she said, though she doubted he'd convince her to leave so easily.

As they moved closer to the gap, another faint noise—this time a soft shuffle of feet—echoed behind them. Both froze, Marcus spinning with his gun raised. The flashlight beam cut through the tunnel, revealing nothing but empty space.

"Eliza…" he began, his voice low and tense.

"I heard it too," she said, her voice tight. She scanned the area with her glasses, but no heat signatures or movement registered. "There's no one here."

"That doesn't mean they're not watching," Marcus replied, his tone grim.

The silence stretched, oppressive and heavy. Finally, Eliza took a step forward, her voice steady despite the unease creeping into her chest. "Let's keep moving. Whatever they're doing, we can't let them scare us off."

Marcus grunted in reluctant agreement, his grip tightening on his weapon. Together, they pressed on, the tunnel's shadows seeming to close in around them. Unseen eyes lingered in the darkness, but Eliza's focus remained on the trail ahead. Whatever waited at the end, they were committed now. There was no turning back.

The tunnel opened into another chamber, smaller and more confined than the last. The air was dense with a damp chill, and Eliza's footsteps echoed faintly as she entered. Her glasses hummed softly as they scanned the room, casting a faint blue glow over the walls.

"Hold up," Marcus said behind her, his voice low. He kept his weapon raised, his eyes scanning the shadows. "This place feels wrong."

"It's definitely something," Eliza murmured, taking a cautious step forward. Her glasses flickered, highlighting faint etchings on the walls. The markings were subtle, hidden beneath years of grime, but they were there—deliberate and precise. Her breath caught as the pattern came into focus.

"What is it?" Marcus asked, moving closer, his tone a mix of curiosity and tension.

She pointed to the wall, her voice tight. "Look at this."

Marcus frowned, tilting his head. "Looks like scratches. So?"

"It's not just scratches," Eliza said, stepping closer. Her gloved hand hovered just above the surface. "It's an emblem. The same one from my mother's journal."

Marcus straightened, his skepticism clear. "The same one? Are you sure?"

Eliza turned to him, her expression resolute. "I'm sure. These markings—they're identical."

Marcus let out a slow breath, lowering his weapon slightly. "All right, so it's a match. What does it mean?"

"It means the Concordant Order was here," she replied, her voice steady despite the weight of her words. She adjusted her glasses, scanning the emblem further. The lenses highlighted faint traces of an energy signature, a soft glow pulsing just beneath the surface. "And recently."

"Recently?" Marcus's brows shot up. "You're telling me this thing is still active? It looks ancient."

"It is ancient," Eliza said, her tone distracted as she continued her scan. "But these energy traces—they're fresh. Someone's been maintaining this."

Marcus leaned against the wall, his face twisting into a skeptical grimace. "Okay, let's say you're right. Why would the Order leave something like this out in the open?"

"They didn't," Eliza replied, turning to face him. "This isn't out in the open. It's hidden in a place they thought no one would look."

"Yeah, well, we're looking," Marcus said, his tone laced with sarcasm. "And I'm guessing they wouldn't be too happy about that."

"Probably not," Eliza admitted, her voice calm but firm. "But that doesn't change the fact that we're here. And this emblem—it's proof. The Order isn't just a theory anymore. It's real."

Marcus sighed, running a hand down his face. "Great. So now we're chasing a secret society through a maze of tunnels. This just keeps getting better."

"Stop complaining and start helping," Eliza shot back. She gestured to the wall. "Take a closer look. See these lines around the emblem?"

He leaned in, squinting. "Yeah. They look… like runes or something."

"They're coordinates," Eliza said, her tone sharper now. "Or instructions. I need to document this."

Marcus straightened, crossing his arms. "Coordinates to what? Another creepy tunnel?"

"Maybe," Eliza said, pulling out her portable scanner. "Or something more significant."

"You're really set on this, aren't you?" Marcus asked, watching her work. "Chasing your mom's ghost through the Order's backyard."

Eliza froze for a fraction of a second, her hand tightening on the scanner. "This isn't about her," she said quietly. "Not entirely."

Marcus's gaze softened, though his voice remained cautious. "You sure about that? Because every time we find something like this, it feels like you're trying to finish what she started."

She didn't respond immediately, her focus remaining on the emblem. The scanner beeped as it captured the markings, preserving the details for further analysis. Finally, she straightened, her expression unreadable.

"Maybe I am," she said softly. "But that doesn't mean it's not worth pursuing."

Marcus shook his head, his frustration mingled with reluctant admiration. "You're impossible, you know that?"

"Good," she replied, sliding the scanner back into her bag. "Let's keep it that way."

He chuckled despite himself, his grip on his weapon relaxing slightly. "All right, Kain. What's next? We following these coordinates to God-knows-where?"

Eliza glanced back at the emblem, the faint glow still pulsing beneath the surface. "Not yet. First, I need to analyze this data.

If we move without knowing what we're walking into, we're asking for trouble."

"Right, because we've been playing it safe so far," Marcus quipped, gesturing to the tunnel behind them. "Fine. Let's head back before this place decides to collapse on us."

Eliza nodded, though her gaze lingered on the emblem for a moment longer. The weight of its presence was undeniable, the connection to her mother's research impossible to ignore. Whatever lay ahead, she knew this was only the beginning.

As they turned to leave, the faint glow of the emblem seemed to dim, as if retreating back into the stone. Eliza felt a chill run down her spine, but she pushed it aside. The Concordant Order was no longer a distant theory. It was here, tangible and dangerous. And she was determined to uncover the truth, no matter where it led.

Chapter 4
The Trap Unfolds

The tunnels stretched endlessly into the darkness, their damp walls narrowing as Eliza and Marcus moved cautiously forward. The faint chemical residue that had guided them so far was still visible in Eliza's glasses, but something else began to emerge—an unsettling glow pulsating faintly on the walls ahead.

"Stop," Eliza said, holding up a hand. Her voice echoed softly in the confined space. She adjusted the settings on her glasses, magnifying the glowing patterns. "There's something up ahead."

Marcus halted, his flashlight sweeping the walls and ceiling. "What now? More scratches? Secret society graffiti?"

"No," Eliza murmured, stepping closer. "This is different."

She moved forward, her glasses picking up more detail as she approached. The glow resolved into intricate symbols etched into the stone walls, each one pulsing with a rhythmic light that seemed almost alive. The patterns were precise, their edges sharp despite the age of the tunnel.

"Eliza," Marcus said, his tone sharp with concern. "What are you seeing?"

"Symbols," she replied, her voice tight with concentration. "Glowing, pulsing... It's like they're sending a message."

Marcus moved to her side, his flashlight now focused on the glowing etchings. "Or trying to scare us off. This feels like an intimidation tactic. Whoever set this up wants to make sure we know we're not welcome."

Eliza shook her head, her gaze fixed on the symbols. "It's more than that. These aren't just warnings—they're deterrents. Calculated, deliberate. Someone went to a lot of trouble to make sure no one got past this point."

Marcus frowned, his skepticism clear. "And yet, here we are."

"Exactly," Eliza said, leaning closer to the wall. Her glasses detected faint energy traces emanating from the symbols. "There's an energy source behind these markings. They're not just decorative—they're functional."

"Functional how?" Marcus asked, his tone laced with sarcasm. "You're telling me these things are booby traps?"

"Maybe," she said, stepping back to study the pattern as a whole. "Or they're meant to guide us—or mislead us."

"Fantastic," Marcus muttered. "So, either we're about to get blown up, or we're walking into the world's worst scavenger hunt."

Eliza ignored his sarcasm, her mind racing. "The pulse is rhythmic," she said, her voice more to herself than to him. "It's almost like a code."

Marcus sighed, crossing his arms. "Of course, it's a code. Why wouldn't it be? Secret societies love their puzzles."

"Because they're effective," Eliza shot back. "Anyone without the right knowledge or tools wouldn't get this far."

"And you have the right knowledge?" Marcus asked, raising an eyebrow.

"I have enough to know these symbols aren't random," she said, scanning the wall again. "The patterns—they match variations in my mother's journal. This isn't just an obstacle. It's a test."

Marcus stepped back, his expression hardening. "A test for what? To see how much danger we're willing to walk into?"

"Maybe," Eliza admitted. "Or to see if we can decipher the meaning."

Marcus groaned, his frustration evident. "Okay, fine. Let's say you're right. What happens if we can't 'decipher the meaning'? Do these things blow up? Release poison gas? Call in reinforcements?"

"I don't know," Eliza said, her tone clipped. "But I'm not planning on failing."

He sighed, running a hand through his hair. "This better be worth it."

Eliza crouched near the base of the wall, her gloved fingers hovering just above the glowing markings. She pulled out her scanner, the device humming softly as it analyzed the energy signature. The results flashed onto her glasses, confirming what she'd suspected—this wasn't natural phosphorescence. It was a synthesized reaction, likely triggered by proximity.

"Triggered by us," she muttered, standing.

"What?" Marcus asked, his tone sharp.

"The glow," she said, pointing to the wall. "It's responding to our presence. We activated it when we entered this section of the tunnel."

Marcus's jaw tightened. "So, they know we're here."

"Possibly," Eliza admitted. "Or it's just a passive system meant to keep intruders out."

"Not comforting," Marcus said flatly.

"It's not supposed to be," Eliza replied, her gaze narrowing as she studied the symbols. "This was designed to make people turn back."

"Well, they've underestimated our stubbornness," Marcus said, adjusting his grip on his flashlight. "What's the plan?"

Eliza stepped back, her mind racing. "We move forward, but carefully. If the energy source powers more than just the glow, there could be traps."

"Traps," Marcus echoed, shaking his head. "Why am I not surprised?"

She shot him a pointed look. "Because you knew what you were getting into when you followed me."

He chuckled despite himself. "Fair enough. Lead the way, genius. But if something explodes, I'm blaming you."

"Noted," Eliza said with a faint smirk. She adjusted her glasses and turned toward the glowing symbols, her resolve hardening. The pulsing light seemed almost hypnotic, urging her forward even as it warned her to stop.

The path ahead was dangerous, but there was no turning back. Whatever the Concordant Order had hidden in these tunnels, she was determined to uncover it—even if it meant walking straight into the trap.

The faint hum of Eliza's glasses filled the tense silence as she scanned the floor. Her focus narrowed on subtle grooves running across the uneven stone surface. She stopped abruptly, holding out a hand to halt Marcus, who nearly collided into her.

"What now?" Marcus hissed, his flashlight darting around the dimly lit tunnel. "Another glowing symbol, or did you find the lost city of gold?"

"Grooves," Eliza said quietly, crouching to inspect them. "They're too regular to be natural. This floor is rigged."

Marcus froze, his expression shifting from frustration to alarm. "Rigged? As in traps?"

"Yes," she replied, her tone clipped. She adjusted her glasses, magnifying the grooves. "See how they form a grid? This isn't random wear and tear. Someone designed this."

"Great," Marcus muttered, taking a cautious step back. "So, what happens if we step on the wrong spot? Spikes? Poison darts? Explosions?"

"I don't know," Eliza admitted, her voice steady but tense. "But I'd rather not find out."

"You and me both," Marcus said, his voice rising slightly. "You couldn't have mentioned traps before we wandered into the death maze?"

Eliza glanced at him, her irritation barely contained. "I didn't know we'd find traps, Marcus. I'm not psychic."

"No, but you're supposed to be the genius," he shot back. "Figuring this stuff out is your thing."

"And I just did," she snapped, standing. "So how about less complaining and more listening?"

Marcus threw up his hands. "Fine. What's the plan, Sherlock?"

She exhaled sharply, scanning the floor ahead. The grooves created a grid that spanned the width of the tunnel, with faint scratches suggesting areas of frequent activation. Her glasses highlighted faint residue near the edges of the grooves—evidence of movement.

"Stay behind me," Eliza instructed, her tone firm. "I'll map out a path through."

"Terrific," Marcus muttered under his breath, his hand instinctively resting on his holstered weapon. "Because this day wasn't stressful enough already."

Eliza ignored him, her focus locked on the task. She took a tentative step forward, her boots carefully avoiding the grooves. The glasses beeped softly as they flagged potential pressure points, guiding her steps like a digital breadcrumb trail.

"Watch where I step," she said, her voice steady. "Don't deviate."

"Easier said than done," Marcus replied, his flashlight beam bouncing as he followed. "You've got tech. I've got… eyes and instinct."

"Then use them," she said, glancing back briefly. "And stay quiet. I need to concentrate."

Marcus grumbled something unintelligible but complied, his footsteps falling in line with hers. The tension in the air was palpable, every movement calculated to avoid disaster.

"You know," Marcus said after a moment, his voice low but sharp, "this feels a little too elaborate for a group that's supposed to be a myth."

Eliza didn't respond immediately, her attention focused on the grid. When she finally spoke, her tone was calm but edged with frustration. "The Concordant Order isn't a myth, Marcus. This is proof of that."

"Oh, I believe you," he said, his sarcasm cutting through the air. "But let me tell you, their recruiting slogan must be something else if it gets people to rig tunnels with death traps."

"They're protecting something," Eliza replied, taking another careful step. "Something they don't want anyone to find."

"Yeah, well, it's working," Marcus muttered, his flashlight flickering briefly as they moved deeper into the tunnel. "Most people would've turned back by now."

"I'm not most people," Eliza said firmly, her gaze locked on the path ahead. "And neither are you."

"Right," Marcus said with a humorless laugh. "Because risking my life in a booby-trapped tunnel is exactly how I wanted to spend my day."

"Do you ever stop talking?" Eliza asked, glancing at him with exasperation.

"Not when we're one wrong step away from becoming human confetti," Marcus shot back.

Eliza sighed, focusing again on the grooves. They were nearing the end of the grid, the grooves tapering off into smooth stone.

The faint residue became more sporadic, indicating they were past the most dangerous section.

"Almost there," she said, her voice quieter now. "Just a few more steps."

"Better be," Marcus muttered, his tone lighter but still tense. "I'm getting real tired of holding my breath."

Eliza reached the end of the grid and turned to face him. "See? Not so bad."

Marcus stepped off the last groove with exaggerated care, his shoulders relaxing slightly. "Yeah, easy for you to say. You've got tech. I've got nerves of steel."

She gave him a faint smirk. "And a lot of complaining."

"Part of my charm," Marcus said with a grin, though his eyes remained wary. "So, what's next? More glowing symbols? Another death trap?"

"We keep moving," Eliza said, scanning the tunnel ahead. "And we stay alert. If they went to this much trouble to secure the path, whatever's at the end is worth finding."

"Or it's just another trap," Marcus countered. "But sure, let's roll the dice."

Eliza gave him a sharp look. "If you're so scared, you can turn back."

He chuckled, shaking his head. "Not a chance, Kain. If you're walking into trouble, someone's got to be there to drag you out."

She didn't respond, though a flicker of gratitude crossed her face. Together, they continued down the tunnel, the weight of the trap behind them and the unknown dangers ahead pressing heavily on their minds.

The air in the tunnel grew colder as the narrow passage gave way to a larger chamber. Eliza paused at the entrance, her forensic glasses adjusting to the new environment. The room was cluttered with remnants of a forgotten past—rusted machinery, stacks of wooden crates, and thick layers of dust that did little to hide the faint glint of something metallic.

Marcus stepped in behind her, his flashlight sweeping the space. "Well, this is cozy," he muttered. "Looks like we've stumbled into someone's storage unit from hell."

Eliza ignored him, her eyes drawn to the crates stacked haphazardly against the far wall. The symbols carved into their sides were unmistakable—the same intricate patterns they'd seen throughout the tunnels and in her mother's journal. She approached cautiously, her heart pounding in her chest.

"Marcus," she said, her voice tight. "Look at this."

He followed her gaze, frowning as he examined the markings. "More of your glowing doodles? Great. What are these, shipping labels for secret societies?"

"They're not just doodles," Eliza said, kneeling beside one of the crates. "These are marks of ownership. Whoever these belonged to—"

"Let me guess," Marcus interrupted, his tone laced with sarcasm. "The Concordant Order?"

Eliza shot him a sharp look but didn't respond. Instead, she pulled out her multi-tool and pried open the lid of the nearest crate. The wood groaned in protest before splintering apart, revealing a trove of aged documents, tarnished metal artifacts, and neatly wrapped bundles of what looked like ledgers.

Marcus crouched beside her, his brows furrowing as he picked up one of the ledgers. "What the hell is this? A shipping manifest?"

Eliza flipped open a ledger, her fingers brushing over the brittle pages. The faded handwriting was precise, detailing locations, dates, and cargo descriptions. Her glasses highlighted key phrases—"secured transport," "classified materials," "direct orders."

"These aren't just shipping manifests," she said, her voice barely above a whisper. "They're records of covert operations. Transport routes, delivery schedules… they were moving something."

Marcus leaned over her shoulder, reading the notes with a growing sense of unease. "Moving what, exactly? Weapons? Drugs?"

"Maybe," Eliza said, scanning the rest of the crate. Her hand hovered over a sealed envelope stamped with the same emblem as the crates. She tore it open, revealing a set of instructions typed on yellowed paper. Her eyes darted across the text, her expression darkening with every line.

"What does it say?" Marcus asked, his tone now serious.

"It's a directive," Eliza replied, holding the paper out for him to see. "Route coordination for 'priority assets.' No specifics on what they were transporting, but the locations…" She pointed to a series of underlined names. "They match sites connected to the councilman."

Marcus straightened, the pieces falling into place. "You think he found out about this? The transport routes, the assets?"

"It's possible," Eliza said, setting the envelope aside. "If he uncovered these operations, that would explain why someone wanted him silenced. He might have known too much."

Marcus paced the room, his flashlight sweeping over the rusted machinery. "So, what are we talking about here? Some kind of underground smuggling ring?"

"Not just smuggling," Eliza said, her tone sharper. "This is organized. Coordinated. These routes—" she gestured to the map in the ledger—"they're too strategic. Whoever was running this had resources, connections. This was more than a side operation."

"And you think the Order's behind it?" Marcus asked, stopping to look at her.

"I don't think," Eliza replied, her voice firm. "I know. These symbols, the way the operations were hidden… it all fits their MO."

Marcus ran a hand down his face, his frustration palpable. "And the councilman? He stumbles onto this, tries to do the right thing, and ends up dead."

"Exactly," Eliza said, her tone heavy. "He was a threat to their secrecy. And if we don't figure out what he uncovered, we'll never understand the full picture."

Marcus let out a low whistle, shaking his head. "Great. So, now we're chasing a murder and unraveling a decades-old conspiracy."

Eliza smirked faintly, though her expression remained tense. "Welcome to my world."

"Lucky me," Marcus muttered, turning his attention to another crate. He pried it open, revealing a collection of outdated communication devices—radios, encrypted recorders, and what looked like old surveillance equipment. "These guys were serious."

"Deadly serious," Eliza said, standing. She scanned the room again, her glasses picking up faint traces of energy near one of the walls. "There's something else here."

Marcus followed her gaze, his hand instinctively moving to his weapon. "Something else? Like what?"

She approached the wall, her fingers tracing a faint outline that glowed under her glasses. It was another emblem, larger than the others, with grooves that suggested it could be moved. "Help me," she said, motioning for Marcus to join her.

Together, they pushed against the emblem. It shifted with a low groan, revealing a hidden compartment embedded in the stone. Inside was a metal cylinder, its surface engraved with the same intricate patterns.

"Care to guess what's in the mystery box?" Marcus asked, his voice tinged with apprehension.

"Something important," Eliza said, carefully removing the cylinder. "Something they didn't want anyone to find."

As she examined it, her mind raced. The Order's intentions were becoming clearer, but the scope of their operations—and their willingness to kill to protect their secrets—left a chill in her chest. Whatever was inside the cylinder, she knew it would be another piece of the puzzle. And she also knew it would put them in even more danger.

"Let's get out of here," Marcus said, his voice breaking her thoughts. "Before they realize we're poking around."

Eliza nodded, slipping the cylinder into her bag. As they left the chamber, the weight of what they'd discovered pressed heavily on her shoulders. The Order's secrets were starting to unravel, and she was determined to see it through, no matter the cost.

The chamber was deathly silent, save for the faint shuffle of Eliza's boots on the stone floor. She scanned the room one last time, her forensic glasses humming softly as they processed the environment. Then, the air shifted—a faint vibration, almost imperceptible at first, pulsing through the chamber like a heartbeat.

"Do you feel that?" she asked, glancing at Marcus.

He paused, his flashlight cutting through the darkness. "Feel what?"

Before she could respond, a faint hum grew louder, low and resonant, reverberating through the walls. Eliza turned sharply toward the source—a symbol carved deep into the stone, its edges glowing brighter with each pulse of the sound.

"Well, that's new," Marcus muttered, his hand instinctively moving to his weapon. "What's it doing?"

"It's reacting to something," Eliza said, stepping closer. The light from the symbol cast eerie shadows across her face as she studied it. "Or someone."

"Let's hope it's not us," Marcus said, his voice tense. "I'm really not in the mood for another trap."

Eliza ignored him, her attention fixed on the symbol. The glow wasn't like the others they'd encountered—it was sharper, more urgent, as if it were trying to communicate something. She adjusted her glasses, analyzing the energy signature. The readings were erratic, the pulsing light now accompanied by a low, almost imperceptible hum.

"Eliza," Marcus said, his voice cutting through the tension. "That thing's getting louder. Tell me you know what it means."

"I don't know yet," she admitted, stepping even closer.

"Yet?" Marcus took a step back. "That's not exactly reassuring."

The symbol's glow intensified, casting the entire chamber in an otherworldly light. Eliza's glasses picked up faint traces of heat emanating from the carving, the energy signature spiking with every pulse.

"This isn't just a marking," she murmured, more to herself than to him. "It's a message."

"Fantastic," Marcus said, his sarcasm laced with unease. "And what's the message? 'Welcome to the Concordant Order'? 'Don't forget to tip your tour guide'?"

Eliza turned to him, her expression grim. "It's a warning."

Marcus frowned, his flashlight beam wavering. "A warning for what?"

"To stay out," Eliza replied, her voice steady despite the growing hum. "Whoever carved this didn't want anyone going further. This is their line in the sand."

"Great," Marcus said, his tone sharp. "So, are we crossing it or what?"

Eliza hesitated, her mind racing. The energy emanating from the symbol was unlike anything she'd seen before—calculated, deliberate, and clearly intended to intimidate. But intimidation wasn't enough to stop her. Not now.

"We have to," she said finally, her voice firm. "Whatever they're hiding, it's too important to turn back."

Marcus let out a frustrated groan. "Of course you'd say that. Why would we stop at the ominous glowing warning sign when we can push our luck even further?"

Eliza gave him a sharp look. "If you're scared, you can stay here."

"Scared?" Marcus scoffed, his grip tightening on his flashlight. "I'm not scared, Eliza. I'm smart. There's a difference."

"Then prove it," she said, turning back to the symbol. "Help me figure out what triggers this. It's not glowing for no reason."

Marcus muttered something under his breath but stepped closer, his flashlight beam steadying as it illuminated the carving. "Fine. But if this thing explodes, I'm haunting you."

Eliza smirked faintly but kept her focus on the symbol. She ran her gloved hand just above its surface, feeling the faint warmth radiating from the grooves. Her glasses highlighted subtle variations in the light's intensity, each pulse slightly different from the last.

"It's encoded," she said, her voice tinged with fascination. "The light patterns—they're a sequence."

Marcus arched a brow. "A sequence for what? Opening a secret door? Activating a death ray?"

"I don't know yet," Eliza replied, her tone sharp. "But it's deliberate. Whoever made this wanted to send a clear message."

"Well, message received," Marcus said, stepping back. "Loud and clear."

The hum grew louder, almost deafening now. The light from the symbol cast jagged patterns across the chamber, making the space feel smaller, more confined. Eliza's chest tightened, but she refused to back down.

"This is more than a warning," she said, her voice rising over the hum. "It's a test. They're daring us to move forward."

Marcus stared at her, his expression unreadable. Then, with a resigned sigh, he holstered his flashlight and crossed his arms. "If you're wrong about this, we're both dead."

"And if I'm right?" Eliza countered, her eyes locked on the glowing symbol.

"Then I'm still blaming you for the stress," Marcus said with a faint grin. "So, what's the plan, fearless leader?"

Eliza took a deep breath, the hum vibrating through her bones. "We figure out what this is protecting. And then we move forward."

Marcus shook his head, a mixture of frustration and admiration in his gaze. "You're relentless, Kain. You know that?"

"Good," she replied, her voice steady. "Because we're not stopping now."

As the symbol pulsed one last time, the hum began to fade, leaving the chamber in an uneasy silence. Whatever lay ahead, Eliza knew they had crossed into territory they couldn't retreat from. The warning was clear, but so was her determination.

Chapter 5
Threats from the Dark

Eliza sat at her workstation, the soft glow of her monitors casting sharp lines across her face. The air in the lab was cool and still, but her mind raced as she sifted through the data they had collected in the tunnels. Her glasses lay on the desk beside her, their lenses smudged from hours of use. The metal cylinder they had found rested nearby, its etched patterns taunting her with unanswered questions.

Her focus was interrupted by the sharp ping of a notification. Then another. And another. She frowned, pulling her attention to the cluster of alerts popping up across her devices.

"Unusual traffic detected," read the first message.

"Eliza Kain, stop now," said the second.

Her frown deepened as more messages flooded her screens. The words were blunt and chilling, each one demanding she abandon her investigation. The sender was anonymous, their presence slipping past her firewalls with unsettling ease.

Her phone buzzed, vibrating violently against the desk. She hesitated before picking it up, but the message there was the same: **STOP. YOU'RE NOT SAFE.**

Eliza's stomach tightened. She typed rapidly into her keyboard, pulling up her system logs to trace the source of the intrusion. The results were almost immediate—and frustratingly vague.

The origin was masked, rerouted through countless servers that made pinpointing it impossible.

"Dammit," she muttered, leaning back in her chair.

A sharp crackle filled the room, and the lights flickered. Her monitors dimmed, then came back on, the eerie glow of the threat messages reflecting off her glasses.

"Eliza!" Marcus's voice barked through her comms channel.

She jumped, fumbling to answer the call. "What?"

"Your lab's camera feeds just went haywire," Marcus said, his tone tight. "I'm looking at static. What's going on over there?"

"Anonymous threats," Eliza replied tersely, her fingers flying across the keyboard as she pulled up the lab's security system. The live feed was a mess of flickering images and static bursts, the once-clear view of the building's perimeter now a distorted blur.

"Well, that's not ominous," Marcus said, his voice crackling slightly through the connection. "You think it's them?"

"Who else?" Eliza said, her jaw tightening. She switched to the internal cameras, only to find the same distortion. "They've breached the system. Whoever this is, they're in deep."

"Do you think they're here? In the building?" Marcus asked, his tone sharpening.

"I don't know," she admitted. "But I'm not waiting to find out."

She moved swiftly across the room, activating the lab's manual lockdown. Heavy metal shutters began to descend over the windows, the faint whir of machinery cutting through the static-laden silence.

"Eliza," Marcus said again, his voice softer this time. "Are you okay?"

"I'm fine," she said curtly, though her racing heart betrayed her words. "This isn't the first time someone's tried to scare me off."

"Yeah, but it's the first time they've gone this far," Marcus replied. "This isn't a prank. They're serious."

"Good," Eliza said, her voice hardening. "Because so am I."

The lights flickered again, plunging the lab into momentary darkness before the backup generator kicked in. Eliza's gaze darted to the cylinder on her desk, the intricate markings suddenly feeling heavier, more dangerous.

"What's your plan?" Marcus asked, his voice grounding her.

She exhaled, forcing herself to focus. "First, I lock this place down. Then I figure out who's behind this and what they want."

"You think it's the Order?" Marcus asked, though they both knew the answer.

"Who else would have the resources to pull this off?" Eliza replied, her fingers tightening around the edge of the desk. "They know I'm onto them. They're trying to scare me off."

"Is it working?" Marcus asked, his tone half-teasing, half-serious.

Eliza's lips twitched into a faint smirk despite the tension. "Not a chance."

The faint sound of static crackled through the lab's speakers, sending a chill down her spine. The screens flickered again, and new messages replaced the older ones.

LEAVE THIS ALONE. YOU WON'T BE WARNED AGAIN.

"Eliza," Marcus said, his voice urgent. "You need to get out of there."

"No," she said firmly. "If I leave, they win. And I'm not letting that happen."

"Eliza—"

"Marcus," she interrupted, her voice sharp but steady. "I've got this."

The line went quiet for a moment before he sighed heavily. "Fine. But if you don't check in every ten minutes, I'm coming over there."

"Deal," she said, already turning her attention back to the screens.

As Marcus ended the call, Eliza began to work methodically, scanning her systems for vulnerabilities and patching breaches where she could. Her fingers moved with practiced efficiency, but her mind buzzed with questions. The messages, the static, the deliberate sabotage—everything pointed to a calculated attempt to scare her off.

And yet, she couldn't shake the feeling that it was more than that. It wasn't just about intimidation. It was a declaration of war.

Her gaze flicked to the cylinder once more, the etched symbols seeming to glow faintly in the dim light. Whatever the Order was protecting, it was worth this level of effort. And if they thought she would back down, they had severely underestimated her.

The lab fell silent again, save for the faint hum of her monitors. Eliza exhaled slowly, her resolve solidifying. They could threaten her, infiltrate her systems, even breach her security—but they wouldn't stop her.

Not now. Not ever.

Eliza's fingers flew over the keyboard, her focus unyielding as she worked to trace the anonymous threats. The room was dimly lit, the glow of her monitors illuminating her face, but the tension in the lab felt as sharp as a knife. The messages had stopped, but the lingering unease in her chest refused to fade. She was close—she could feel it—but whoever was behind this was as meticulous as they were relentless.

The loud buzz of the lab's intercom broke her concentration, making her flinch. She glanced toward the security feed, still scrambled with static. Her eyes narrowed as a voice called from the other side of the locked door.

"Eliza! Open up!" Marcus's voice rang out, sharp and urgent. "It's me!"

With a sigh, she stood, her mind still racing with possibilities. She hit the button to release the lock, and the door slid open, revealing Marcus with a tense expression. He stepped inside, glancing around the room as if expecting trouble to leap from the shadows.

"You okay?" he asked, his voice low but edged with concern.

"I'm fine," Eliza replied, returning to her desk. "What are you doing here?"

Marcus gestured to the chaotic security feed on her monitors. "I saw the static on your cameras, heard you weren't answering your comms, and figured I'd check in. Looks like I made the right call."

"I was busy," she said curtly, her fingers resuming their work on the keyboard. "They breached the system, and I'm trying to trace the source."

Marcus groaned, dragging a hand through his hair. "Eliza, are you serious? Someone just hacked into your lab, sent you threats, and you're worried about tracing them? You need to leave."

"I'm not leaving," she said firmly, her eyes locked on the screen. "Not until I figure out who's behind this."

"Dammit, Eliza," Marcus snapped, stepping closer. "This isn't just some academic challenge. These people aren't playing games. They're dangerous."

"I know that," she shot back, her voice rising. "But walking away isn't going to make them less dangerous. If anything, it'll just give them more power."

Marcus stared at her, frustration flashing in his eyes. "You think you can outsmart them? These aren't amateurs. They got into your system like it was child's play. What makes you think they won't come after you next?"

"That's exactly why I need to do this," Eliza said, her tone unwavering. "If they're willing to go this far, it means I'm onto something. Something they don't want me to find."

He sighed, leaning heavily against the edge of her desk. "And what happens if they come for you? In person? You think your locks and gadgets are going to stop them?"

"They'll have to get through me first," she said coldly.

Marcus let out a bitter laugh. "Oh, that's comforting. You're brilliant, Eliza, but you're not invincible."

"I don't need to be invincible," she countered, her voice sharp. "I need to finish what I started."

"For what?" Marcus demanded, his voice rising. "For the councilman? For your mother? Is any of this worth your life?"

Her hands paused, hovering over the keyboard. For a moment, her resolve wavered, but the weight of the cylinder on her desk brought her focus back. She turned to face him, her expression hard.

"Yes," she said quietly. "It is."

Marcus shook his head, the fight draining from his posture. "You're impossible, you know that?"

"Good," she said, turning back to her work. "Because I'm not giving up."

He sighed, pacing the room. "At least let me help. Two heads are better than one, right?"

"You're not exactly a tech wizard, Marcus," she said, a faint smirk tugging at her lips.

"No," he admitted, "but I'm great at pointing out when you're being reckless."

She rolled her eyes but didn't argue. "Fine. Keep an eye on the cameras. If they're watching, I want to know about it."

"Done," he said, pulling up a chair and grabbing her tablet to access the security logs. "But if I see anything suspicious, we're leaving. No arguments."

"Deal," she replied, though the determination in her voice left little room for compromise.

As the room fell into a tense silence, the weight of the threats hung heavy between them. Eliza's fingers moved steadily across the keyboard, her focus unbroken despite Marcus's presence. She was close—she could feel it—and she wasn't going to let fear stop her.

Marcus glanced at her, his jaw tightening. "For the record, I still think this is a bad idea."

"Noted," Eliza said, her tone distracted but firm. "Now let me work."

He sighed again, leaning back in his chair. "You better know what you're doing, Kain."

"I always do," she said, her eyes locked on the screen. But even as she spoke, the flicker of unease in her chest refused to fade.

Eliza's fingers hesitated over the keyboard, the glow of her monitors reflecting in her tense expression. She had been so close—another keystroke, another line of code, and she might have broken through the web of rerouted signals masking the origin of the threats. But now, every screen in the lab flickered simultaneously, her command lines replaced by a stark, ominous message.

"You won't leave this case alive."

The words blazed across every monitor, the harsh white text pulsating against a black background. The room seemed colder, quieter, as though the threat itself had drained the air.

"Eliza," Marcus said, his voice low and steady, cutting through the tension. He stood behind her, his arms crossed tightly over his chest. "We're leaving. Now."

Her jaw tightened, her hands balling into fists as she stared at the screens. The message burned into her mind, and though she felt her pulse quicken, she refused to let the fear show.

"I'm not running," she said finally, her voice quiet but firm. "This is exactly what they want."

"And what do you think happens if you stay?" Marcus countered, stepping closer. "You think they're bluffing? You think this is just a scare tactic?"

"They're escalating," she admitted, turning her gaze toward him. "But if I leave now, I lose everything. The evidence, the momentum. They win."

"This isn't about winning or losing anymore," Marcus said, his frustration breaking through his usual calm. "This is about keeping you alive. That message wasn't a suggestion, Eliza. It's a promise."

She didn't respond immediately, her eyes flicking back to the monitors. The message continued to pulse, each flicker tightening the knot in her stomach. The Concordant Order wasn't playing games anymore. They wanted her silenced.

Finally, she stood, her movements sharp and deliberate. "Fine. I'll leave. But I'm taking everything I need with me."

Marcus exhaled, relief flickering across his face. "Good. Let's move fast."

Eliza grabbed a sturdy, weatherproof bag from beneath her workstation, quickly packing it with the most critical pieces of evidence: the cylinder from the tunnels, her mother's journal, portable drives loaded with encrypted files, and her forensic glasses. Each item felt heavier than the last, the weight of their importance pressing down on her shoulders.

"You sure that's everything?" Marcus asked, glancing toward the screens. The message hadn't changed, and the flickering light cast ominous shadows across the room.

"It's enough," Eliza said, zipping the bag. She hesitated for a moment before pulling a small device from her desk—a portable jammer designed to block tracking signals. She activated it, the faint hum reassuring her that at least one layer of protection was in place.

Marcus moved to the door, his hand hovering near his holstered weapon. "I'll cover you. Stay close."

She nodded, slinging the bag over her shoulder and stepping toward him. As they reached the exit, the lights in the lab flickered violently, plunging the room into darkness for a moment before the emergency backup kicked in. The message on the monitors was gone, replaced by static.

"They're not done," Marcus said grimly, opening the door and scanning the hallway. "Let's go."

The two moved quickly through the building, their footsteps echoing in the empty corridors. Eliza's mind raced with half-formed plans, her determination battling the nagging fear that the Order's reach extended further than she had anticipated.

"Where are we going?" Marcus asked as they exited the building and stepped into the cool night air.

"Somewhere secure," she said, her voice steady despite the tension in her chest. "I have a safehouse a few miles from here. We can regroup there."

He nodded, his expression hard. "Good. But after this, we do things my way. No more taking risks without backup."

Eliza didn't argue, her focus already on the next steps. The threat was real, and the Order wasn't going to stop until she was silenced. But if they thought she would give up so easily, they had underestimated her resolve.

As they reached Marcus's car, she slid into the passenger seat, her bag clutched tightly against her chest. The message replayed in her mind, its finality chilling. **"You won't leave this case alive."**

But as the engine roared to life and they sped away from the lab, a steely determination replaced her fear. She wouldn't just leave the case alive—she would see it through to the end. No matter what it cost.

The heavy metal door of the lab groaned shut behind them, sealing the darkened room in silence. Eliza adjusted the strap of her bag, her mind still racing as she followed Marcus into the night. The cold air was sharp against her skin, a stark contrast to the sterile chill of the lab. She glanced back, her stomach tightening as the lab's exterior lights flickered and went out completely.

"Eliza," Marcus said, his tone sharp, snapping her out of her thoughts. "We need to move."

She nodded but paused, her gaze fixed on the darkened building. "They're not just trying to scare me," she said quietly, more to herself than to him.

"No kidding," Marcus replied, his flashlight cutting through the darkness. "They just wiped your lab off the grid. What were you expecting, an apology note?"

"I wasn't expecting them to be this bold," she shot back, her voice tinged with frustration. "This is a declaration."

"Yeah, and you're the one they're declaring war on," Marcus said, stepping closer. "Come on, Eliza. We can analyze their motives later. Right now, we need to get you out of here."

She hesitated, her eyes still on the lifeless building. "I can't believe I let this happen."

Marcus groaned, his patience wearing thin. "You didn't 'let' anything happen. These people are pros, and they've clearly been planning this. Don't beat yourself up when they're the ones pulling the strings."

"I should've been more prepared," she insisted, her jaw tightening. "I should've anticipated this."

"And what? Built a fortress? Installed anti-hacker turrets?" Marcus stepped in front of her, forcing her to meet his gaze. "Listen to me: This isn't your fault. But if you stand here blaming yourself, you're giving them exactly what they want. Is that what you want?"

"No," she admitted, her voice barely above a whisper.

"Then let's go," Marcus said firmly. "We regroup. We figure out our next move. But first, we get somewhere safe."

Eliza nodded reluctantly, turning away from the lab. They made their way toward Marcus's car, their footsteps crunching against the gravel. As they reached the vehicle, a faint rumble echoed in the distance. Eliza froze, her instincts kicking in.

"Do you hear that?" she asked, her voice low.

Marcus tensed, his hand moving to his weapon. "Yeah. And I don't like it."

They turned toward the lab just in time to see a burst of light flash through the windows, followed by a loud *crack*. A plume of smoke rose into the air, and the faint orange glow of fire lit up the night.

"They just destroyed it," Marcus said, his voice laced with disbelief. "They're covering their tracks."

Eliza's heart sank as the realization hit her. Everything she hadn't packed, every piece of data she hadn't saved, was gone. Her lab—her safe haven—was a smoldering ruin. But beneath the shock, anger began to rise.

"They think this will stop me," she said, her voice cold. "They think they can scare me off by erasing everything I've built."

"Eliza," Marcus warned, his tone cautious. "Don't—"

"They're wrong," she interrupted, turning to face him. Her eyes burned with determination. "This doesn't end here. I won't let them win."

Marcus sighed, running a hand through his hair. "You're relentless. You know that?"

"It's the only way to beat them," she said simply. "If I give up now, they've already won."

"And if you keep pushing?" Marcus asked, his frustration evident. "What happens when they come after you again? Or worse?"

"I'll be ready," she said, her voice steady. "Next time, they won't catch me off guard."

"Next time?" Marcus repeated, shaking his head. "Eliza, they just blew up your lab. What makes you think there won't be a next time?"

"Because I'm not giving them the chance," she replied. "This isn't just about me anymore, Marcus. It's about the truth."

He stared at her, his expression a mix of exasperation and admiration. Finally, he let out a resigned sigh. "Fine. But if you're not going to back down, at least promise me you'll be smart about it."

"I always am," she said, a faint smirk breaking through her determined expression.

"That's debatable," he muttered, opening the car door. "Now, get in. We need to put some distance between us and this place before they send more fireworks."

Eliza climbed into the passenger seat, clutching her bag tightly. As the car sped away from the burning lab, she felt the weight of the night settle heavily on her shoulders. She had lost her lab, her tools, and her sense of security. But she still had the evidence—and her resolve.

The flames in the rearview mirror grew smaller as they drove, but Eliza's determination burned brighter than ever. The Order had made their move, and now it was her turn to respond. This wasn't over. Not by a long shot.

Chapter 6
Echoes of Betrayal

The crime scene was a tableau of death and precision, set against the grim backdrop of an abandoned warehouse on the edge of Caelum Heights. The victim lay sprawled on the cold concrete floor, his lifeless eyes fixed on the vaulted ceiling above. Around him, symbols were etched into the ground in perfect symmetry, glowing faintly under the ultraviolet light of Dr. Eliza Kain's forensic glasses.

Eliza knelt by the body, her movements slow and deliberate. The victim was a man in his late thirties, dressed in a suit that hinted at wealth but carried none of the usual arrogance of power. His hands were placed carefully over his chest, clutching a single object—a key carved from obsidian.

"Cipher again," muttered Marcus Hale from behind her, his voice low and filled with unease. He leaned against a rusted support beam, his hand resting on the grip of his gun. "That makes three now, doesn't it?"

"Three," Eliza confirmed, her voice calm but focused. Her glasses scanned the scene, overlaying data in her field of vision. "But this one's different. The symbols are more intricate."

Marcus frowned, stepping closer. "Different how?"

She gestured to the glowing etchings surrounding the body. "Look at the precision. The spacing between the lines. This isn't just a message—it's a code. They're trying to tell us something."

"Tell us or taunt us?" Marcus asked, his tone dark.

"Both, probably," she said, her gaze narrowing as her glasses highlighted faint traces of a residue smeared along the edges of the markings. "Hand me the scanner."

Marcus retrieved the device from her bag, passing it to her without a word. She switched it on, the soft hum of the scanner filling the cavernous space as she swept it over the symbols.

"What do you see?" he asked, crouching beside her.

"Chemical traces," she replied, watching as the scanner displayed a series of complex compounds. "Same as the other two scenes. It's synthetic, but it's not a match for anything in the database. Whoever made this—whatever made this—knows how to stay ahead of us."

"Great," Marcus muttered. "Because what we needed was a murder and a chemistry lesson."

Eliza didn't respond, her focus shifting to the obsidian key in the victim's hands. She reached for it carefully, her gloves brushing against the cold, smooth surface.

"Wait," Marcus said, his hand on her wrist. "You sure that's safe?"

She glanced at him, her expression calm. "If it were rigged, it would've triggered already. They wanted us to find it."

Reluctantly, he let go, and Eliza lifted the key from the victim's hands. It was heavier than she expected, its edges sharp and its surface carved with more symbols—smaller, more intricate than those on the ground.

"These markings," she murmured, holding the key up to her glasses for a closer look. "They match the ones in the tunnels."

Marcus cursed softly under his breath. "The tunnels again. You think this guy was connected to the Order?"

"Almost definitely," she said, rising to her feet. Her gaze swept the room, taking in every detail—the scuffed floors, the faint impressions of footprints leading to and from the body. "This wasn't just a killing. It was a message. They're trying to warn us off."

"Warn you, you mean," Marcus said, his voice heavy. "You're the one they're targeting."

She didn't deny it, her jaw tightening as she placed the key in a protective case. "And I'm not backing down."

He stood as well, crossing his arms. "You're playing a dangerous game, Eliza. These people don't just kill—they make examples."

"I know," she said, her tone firm. "That's why I have to stop them."

He sighed, glancing back at the body. "You've got the tools, the smarts. But we need more than that. If this is about the Order, we're going to need allies."

Eliza didn't reply immediately, her mind already racing with connections and possibilities. She stepped closer to the symbols, her scanner beeping softly as it processed the data.

"What do you think it means?" Marcus asked after a moment.

She straightened, her gaze unwavering. "It's not just a code—it's a map. They're leading us somewhere."

"And you're planning to follow it?"

"I don't have a choice," she said, turning back to the body. "If we don't, more people will die. And next time, it might not just be someone we don't know."

Marcus stared at her, his expression a mix of frustration and admiration. "You're relentless, you know that?"

She almost smiled. "I've been told."

As they packed up their equipment and prepared to leave, the symbols on the ground seemed to pulse faintly, as if mocking her determination. Eliza didn't look back. The path forward was dangerous, but she was already too deep to turn away.

The hum of Eliza's lab was a familiar comfort, the faint whir of analytical machines filling the silence as she worked. Her glasses displayed the decoded fragments from the crime scene, lines of symbols and their potential meanings scrolling in her field of vision. The obsidian key lay in a sealed case on her desk, its markings still defying a clear translation.

Her phone buzzed sharply, breaking her focus. She glanced at the screen. No number. No caller ID.

"Perfect," she muttered, swiping to answer.

At first, there was silence. Then a voice emerged, low and smooth, each word measured with deliberate precision.

"You see the pattern, don't you, Dr. Kain?"

Eliza's blood ran cold, her grip tightening on the phone. "Who is this?"

"You already know who I am," the voice replied, unfazed by her demand. "But names are irrelevant, aren't they? What matters is the work."

"What work?" she asked, her voice sharp. "You mean the murders? The symbols? The threats?"

"All pieces of the same puzzle," the voice said. "And you're so close to understanding. I can see it in your movements, your deductions. You've begun to unravel the Order's legacy."

She bristled, leaning forward in her chair. "If you think I'm going to let you keep killing people, you don't know me as well as you think."

There was a faint chuckle, low and cold. "You misunderstand, Dr. Kain. I don't kill out of chaos or malice. My actions are deliberate, calculated. Each death serves a purpose."

"A purpose?" she snapped. "You're just another murderer hiding behind philosophy."

"No," the voice countered, its tone hardening. "I'm an architect. And so are you, in your own way. We both seek the truth, though you cling to outdated notions of morality. Tell me, have you found the connection yet? Between the marks, the tunnels, the keys?"

Eliza's heart pounded as the implications of the question hit her. "What are you trying to say?"

"You already see the pattern," the voice said, softer now. "Follow it. The answers lie where the symbols converge. The Order's secrets, their lies—they're all waiting for you."

Her breath caught. "Why? Why tell me this? What's your angle?"

"My angle?" the voice repeated, amusement creeping into its tone. "Let's call it… alignment of interests. You and I are not so different, Dr. Kain. You want justice. I want truth. To achieve either, the Order must fall."

Eliza's hand tightened around the phone. "And you think I'm going to help you?"

"I think," the voice said, "you'll do whatever it takes to uncover the truth. Even if it means walking a dangerous path."

The line clicked, and the call ended abruptly. Before Eliza could react, the phone screen glitched, the call log erasing itself before her eyes.

"Damn it," she hissed, slamming the phone down.

The lab door creaked open, and Marcus stepped in, a cup of coffee in hand. "That didn't sound like a friendly conversation."

Eliza shot him a look, her chest heaving. "It wasn't."

He set the coffee down, his brow furrowing. "What's going on?"

"A message," she said, pacing the length of the room. "From Cipher."

Marcus stiffened. "Cipher? What did they say?"

"They said I'm close. That I see the pattern, that I need to follow it," she said, her voice clipped.

Marcus frowned, leaning against the counter. "And you believe them?"

"I don't know," she admitted. "But they know too much—about me, about the investigation. They're trying to manipulate me, but I can't tell why."

"To steer you in their direction," Marcus said. "Whatever they're planning, they want you involved."

"Exactly," she said, stopping mid-pace. "But why? What's their endgame?"

Marcus crossed his arms, his jaw tightening. "Could be a trap. Could be their way of testing you. Either way, we can't take anything they say at face value."

"I know," she said, her voice quiet but firm. "But they're right about one thing—I'm close. I can feel it."

Marcus sighed. "You're not seriously thinking about following their lead, are you?"

Eliza met his gaze, her expression unwavering. "If it gets me closer to the truth, I have to. But I'm not doing it their way—I'm doing it mine."

He nodded reluctantly, his trust in her evident despite his unease. "Just promise me you'll be careful. Cipher's not just playing a game—they're making the rules."

"I know," she said, turning back to her workstation. "But rules can be broken."

As she sat down, the faint hum of her machines filled the room again. The symbols on her screen seemed to pulse with new meaning, their intricate patterns whispering secrets she was determined to uncover. Cipher's words lingered in her mind, a challenge she couldn't ignore.

Follow it.

Eliza spread the map from the chemical plant across the surface of her workstation, smoothing its worn edges with meticulous care. The faded lines and cryptic markings had haunted her since the night she found it, each one hinting at something far bigger than she had imagined. Now, with the latest crime scene photos displayed on her monitor, the pieces were beginning to fall into place.

Marcus stood nearby, arms crossed as he sipped his coffee. "You've been staring at that thing for hours. Got anything yet?"

She didn't answer immediately, her focus locked on the glowing symbols overlaying the map through her forensic glasses. The intricate patterns from the crime scene formed a distinct grid that mirrored the layout on the map.

"Here," she said finally, pointing to a section near the map's center. "This symbol—it's identical to the one we found at the warehouse."

Marcus set his coffee down and leaned over her shoulder. "That's... what, the fifth match?"

"Sixth," she corrected. "And they're not just matches—they're markers. Look at how they're positioned. Each one lines up perfectly with a site tied to the Order: the factory, the tunnels, the councilman's office."

He frowned, studying the map. "So you're saying all these places are connected?"

"I'm saying they're part of a larger system," she said, her voice steady with conviction. "This map isn't just a record of locations—it's a network. And the symbols are the key."

Marcus let out a low whistle, rubbing the back of his neck. "Okay, but what's the endgame here? Why leave a map like this lying around?"

Eliza glanced up at him, her expression grim. "It wasn't left lying around. It was planted—for someone who knew what to look for."

"And that someone is you," Marcus said, his tone tinged with frustration.

"Maybe," she admitted, turning her attention back to the map. "But whoever left it didn't expect me to find this." She pointed to a specific marking on the lower corner of the map, circled faintly in faded ink.

"What is that?" Marcus asked, squinting.

"An archive," Eliza said. "According to the notes my glasses have reconstructed, it's an underground vault in the Old Quarter. If I'm right, this is where the Order stored their most sensitive records."

Marcus raised an eyebrow. "And you think those records are still there?"

"I do," she said, her voice firm. "This map was made long before the Order went underground—metaphorically, at least. If they abandoned this archive, it's because they thought no one would ever find it."

"Or because it's a trap," Marcus pointed out.

Eliza smirked faintly. "Everything's a trap with the Order. That doesn't mean we ignore it."

He sighed, running a hand through his hair. "So let me get this straight. You've got a centuries-old map, glowing murder symbols, and a possible death trap in the Old Quarter. What's next? Dragons?"

"Very funny," she said, rolling up the map. "This is our first real lead, Marcus. If we don't follow it, we're back to chasing shadows."

"And if we do, we might be walking straight into Cipher's hands," he countered.

She paused, the weight of his words settling over her. "Cipher wants me to follow the pattern. But that doesn't mean I'm doing it for them. If this archive exists, it's a chance to find out what they're really after—and how to stop them."

Marcus leaned back against the counter, watching her carefully. "You're set on this, aren't you?"

"I don't have a choice," she said, slipping the map into her bag. "The Order's been running this city from the shadows for too long. This might be the only way to bring them into the light."

He exhaled sharply, his jaw tightening. "Fine. But if we're doing this, we're doing it together. No running off on your own, no late-night heroics. Got it?"

She glanced at him, her expression softening. "Got it."

The tension in the room eased slightly, though the weight of their mission remained heavy.

As they prepared to leave, Eliza's thoughts raced ahead. The symbols on the map, the markers on the ground—they were all pieces of a puzzle she was determined to solve. Somewhere beneath the cobbled streets of the Old Quarter, the Order's secrets lay buried. And she intended to unearth them, no matter the cost.

The glow of the lab's screens cast faint reflections on the glass surfaces of the equipment, their rhythmic hum the only sound until Marcus broke the silence.

"You're really going to do this, aren't you?" he said, his tone low but edged with frustration.

Eliza didn't look up from the map spread across her workstation. "What choice do I have?"

Marcus stepped closer, crossing his arms. "You always have a choice, Eliza. And right now, you're choosing to walk straight into a trap."

She finally glanced at him, her expression calm but unyielding. "We don't know it's a trap."

"Come on," he said, exhaling sharply. "A centuries-old map suddenly lines up perfectly with a murder scene that just so happens to match Cipher's message? You really think that's a coincidence?"

"No," she admitted, her tone even. "But that doesn't mean we ignore it. If this archive is real, it could hold the key to understanding what the Order is planning—and how to stop them."

"And if it's not real?" Marcus countered. "If it's just another one of Cipher's games? What then?"

Eliza didn't answer, her fingers tracing the edge of the map as though it could offer her some reassurance.

"That's what I thought," Marcus said, his voice hardening. "You're not thinking this through. Cipher doesn't leave breadcrumbs out of the goodness of their heart. This isn't a lead—it's a leash."

Her head snapped up, her gaze sharp. "I'm not their pawn, Marcus."

"Then stop acting like it!" he said, his voice rising. "You keep saying you're following the evidence, but all I see is you doing exactly what they want. They're pulling the strings, and you're dancing right along."

She stood abruptly, the tension in her body mirroring his. "Do you think I don't know that? Do you think I don't see the risks? But what do you want me to do? Walk away? Let more people die while we wait for a safer option?"

"I want you to be smart," he said, stepping closer. "I want you to stop treating this like it's just another case. It's not. These people aren't just killers—they're manipulators. They'll use you, break you, and toss you aside when they're done."

"I'm not afraid of them," she said, her voice low but steady.

"Maybe you should be," he shot back.

They stared at each other, the air between them charged with unspoken words.

"You think I don't know what's at stake?" she said finally, her tone quieter but no less intense. "Every step I take, I'm aware of the risk. But I can't stop. Not now. Not when we're this close."

Marcus shook his head, his frustration giving way to something softer—something like worry. "Close to what, Eliza? The truth? Or an early grave?"

Her silence was answer enough, and it only deepened the rift between them.

"You're shutting me out," he said, his voice softer now but no less strained. "Again. You always do this when things get hard. You think you have to carry it all on your own, but you don't. You have me. You've always had me."

Eliza's gaze faltered, the weight of his words pressing against the walls she had built around herself. "I know," she said quietly.

"Then let me in," he said, stepping even closer. "Let me help you. We can find another way, together. But not like this. Not chasing clues left by someone who clearly doesn't have your best interests in mind."

She hesitated, her hands resting on the edge of the table as though bracing herself. "I need to see this through, Marcus."

"And I need you alive to do it," he said, his voice breaking slightly.

The crack in his resolve nearly broke her, but she pushed the feeling aside, locking it behind the same door she always did when things became too much. "I'll be careful," she said finally, though they both knew the words carried little weight.

"That's not good enough," he said, his frustration resurfacing.

"It has to be," she replied, her voice firm again.

Marcus stepped back, shaking his head. "You're impossible, you know that?"

"I've been told," she said, her lips curving into a faint, humorless smile.

He didn't return it. "You're not going to listen to me, are you?"

"I'm listening," she said, meeting his gaze. "But I can't stop."

Marcus stared at her for a long moment before letting out a heavy sigh. "Fine. Do what you have to do. But don't expect me to stand here and watch you destroy yourself."

She flinched at the words, but her resolve didn't waver. "I don't expect you to understand, Marcus. But I have to do this."

He shook his head again, turning toward the door. "Just don't forget who's in your corner, Eliza. Because you're going to need someone when all of this falls apart."

The door clicked shut behind him, leaving her alone with the map and her thoughts. She sank back into her chair, the weight of the moment pressing down on her. Marcus's words echoed in her mind, but she shoved them aside.

She didn't have the luxury of doubt. Not now.

With a deep breath, she turned back to the symbols on the map. The path ahead was dangerous, but it was one she had to take—no matter the cost.

Chapter 7
Fragments of the Past

The smell of smoke hit Eliza the moment she stepped into the hallway outside her lab. It was sharp, acrid, and unmistakably fresh. Her pulse quickened as she broke into a run, the echoes of her boots ricocheting off the walls.

The corridor was dimmer than usual, the emergency lights casting a dull red glow. Her stomach clenched as she reached the lab door, which hung slightly ajar, the lock bent and mangled.

"Marcus," she barked into her comm device, slamming the door open. "Are you near the lab?"

Static crackled for a moment before his voice came through, strained. "I was heading your way. Why? What's wrong?"

"Someone's been here," she said, coughing as smoke billowed into the hallway.

Inside, the lab was in chaos. Her carefully organized workstations were upended, papers and tools scattered across the floor. The hum of her equipment had been replaced with an eerie silence, save for the occasional spark of frayed wires.

She stepped inside cautiously, scanning the room with her forensic glasses. Her heart sank as she saw the shattered remains of her analyzer on the floor, the glass from its casing glinting in the dim light.

"Eliza!" Marcus appeared in the doorway, his expression shifting from concern to alarm as he took in the scene. "What the hell happened?"

"Sabotage," she said, her voice tight.

He moved beside her, his hand instinctively resting on the grip of his gun. "By who?"

Eliza knelt by the main workstation, her fingers brushing over a strange symbol carved into the surface. It was the same symbol from the warehouse crime scene, etched with precision into the wood.

"The Shadows," she said grimly.

Marcus frowned, crouching beside her. "And they left their calling card. Great. That's not ominous at all."

"They didn't just vandalize," she said, scanning the room again. Her forensic glasses highlighted several missing pieces of equipment and storage units. "They took the evidence."

"All of it?"

She nodded, standing and turning toward the overturned shelves. "The map, the key, even the residue samples. Everything we've collected—it's gone."

Marcus swore under his breath, running a hand through his hair. "So they're not just sending a message. They're covering their tracks."

"Exactly," she said, moving toward the central console. The screen was cracked, the faintest hint of static flickering across its surface. She tapped a few keys, her fingers moving quickly despite the damage.

"What are you doing?" Marcus asked, his eyes scanning the room for any signs of movement.

"Checking the security feed," she said. "If they're smart, they'll have wiped it. But maybe they missed something."

The console sputtered, lines of corrupted data streaming across the screen. Eliza cursed under her breath.

"Nothing?" Marcus asked.

She shook her head. "They covered their tracks here, too."

His jaw tightened. "This isn't just about the evidence, Eliza. They're trying to rattle you."

"Then they underestimated me," she said, her voice cold. "This doesn't end here."

Marcus straightened, his frustration evident. "You keep saying that like you're invincible. But look around. They just tore through your lab like it was nothing, and they left us with squat. What's the plan now?"

She stared at the symbol carved into her workstation, her mind racing. "They didn't just take the evidence—they left this."

"And what does that tell us?" Marcus asked, crossing his arms.

"That they want me to follow them," she said, her tone sharp.

Marcus frowned. "Follow them where?"

"I don't know yet," she admitted, turning toward him. "But this wasn't random. They're trying to guide me, just like Cipher. The question is why."

"Maybe because they know you'll bite," Marcus said, his voice tinged with anger. "And maybe that's exactly what they want."

She met his gaze, her expression hard. "What's the alternative? Let them walk away with everything we've been working toward? Let them win?"

"I'm not saying back down," he said, his voice softening slightly. "I'm saying be smart. We're up against people who clearly have the upper hand. If we're going to take them on, we need more than guts and determination."

Eliza took a deep breath, the weight of his words sinking in. "You're right," she said finally. "But I'm not letting this go. We find them. We stop them. And we take back what they stole."

Marcus nodded, though his worry was clear. "All right. But whatever happens next, we do it together. No running off on your own. Agreed?"

"Agreed," she said, though the look in her eyes hinted at her resolve to do whatever it took—no matter the cost.

As the smoke began to dissipate, the lab felt emptier than ever. The Shadows had taken more than evidence—they had taken her sense of control. But they had also left a trail, however cryptic, and Eliza was determined to follow it.

This wasn't over. Not by a long shot.

The clamor of destruction still echoed in Eliza's ears as she darted through the shattered remains of her lab. Smoke clung to the air, acrid and stinging, as her glasses flickered with alerts about hazardous particulates. Her mind raced, sifting through the chaos for any semblance of clarity, when a sharp sound—like a crack of lightning—cut through the air.

"Get down!" Marcus's voice roared behind her.

Before she could react, something heavy slammed into her, knocking her to the floor. Her breath left her in a rush as Marcus shielded her with his body. A second blast rang out, the shockwave reverberating through the walls.

"Marcus!" she gasped, twisting beneath him. "Are you—"

"I'm fine," he grunted, his voice tight. But as he shifted, she saw his face pale, his jaw clenched against pain.

Her heart sank. "You're not fine."

He didn't respond, his weight easing off her just enough for her to scramble free. That's when she saw it—blood seeping through his jacket, spreading across his side.

"Damn it, Marcus!" she snapped, pressing her hands to the wound. "Why didn't you—"

"Because you needed cover," he interrupted, his voice rough but steady. "And I wasn't about to let you get blown to pieces."

"You idiot," she said, her tone wavering between anger and fear. "You're bleeding out!"

He smirked faintly, though it lacked his usual humor. "It's just a scratch."

Eliza's forensic glasses scanned the injury, highlighting the jagged edges of the shrapnel embedded in his side. "It's not just a scratch," she said through gritted teeth. "We need to stop the bleeding."

"No time," Marcus said, trying to push himself upright. "If they're still here—"

"They're gone," she said firmly, grabbing a nearby first-aid kit from the debris. "And if you keep moving, you'll be gone, too. So stay still and let me work."

For once, he didn't argue, though his breathing grew heavier as she cleaned the wound. The tension in the room was palpable, broken only by the distant hum of the lab's failing systems.

"You don't have to do this, you know," Marcus said after a moment, his voice quieter now.

"Do what?" she asked, focusing on extracting the shrapnel.

"Play hero," he said. "You could've walked away from all this—the Order, Cipher, the danger. But you didn't."

She glanced at him, her expression tight. "And what would I have done? Let them win? Let them destroy more lives?"

"You could've lived," he said simply.

She shook her head, her hands working quickly. "Living doesn't mean much if you're running away."

A soft chuckle escaped him, though it turned into a wince. "You're stubborn, you know that?"

"You've mentioned it," she said, her voice softening slightly.

For a moment, silence settled between them as she finished dressing the wound. Marcus's breathing steadied, though his face was still pale, the lines of pain etched deeply into his features.

"Eliza," he said quietly, breaking the silence.

She paused, looking at him. His gaze was steady, even in his weakened state.

"You can't keep doing this alone," he said. "You think pushing me away keeps me safe, but it doesn't. It just makes things harder—for both of us."

Her throat tightened, the weight of his words hitting harder than she wanted to admit. "I wasn't trying to push you away," she said softly.

"You were," he said, his voice unwavering. "And I get it. You think if you keep me at arm's length, I won't get hurt. But newsflash: I'm here, Eliza. I'm in this. And I'm not going anywhere."

She swallowed hard, her hands stilling against the bandages. "Marcus—"

"No," he interrupted, his voice firmer now. "Listen to me. I'm with you in this, whether you like it or not. You don't get to decide that for me."

Her eyes stung, but she blinked back the tears threatening to spill. "You don't understand what it's like—feeling responsible for everything that happens to the people around you."

"Of course I understand," he said, his tone softening. "I've been watching you carry that weight for years. But you don't have to. You have me. And I'm not letting you do this alone."

For a long moment, she didn't respond. The chaos around them seemed to fade, leaving just the two of them in the ruined lab.

"Okay," she said finally, her voice barely above a whisper.

Marcus raised an eyebrow. "Okay?"

She nodded, her hands tightening slightly on the bandages. "Okay. I'll stop trying to keep you out."

A faint smile tugged at the corner of his mouth. "About time."

Her lips twitched in response, though her expression remained serious. "But if you pull a stunt like this again, I swear—"

"Yeah, yeah," he said, his voice lighter now. "I'll let you take the next hit."

She rolled her eyes, standing and offering him a hand. "Come on. Let's get you out of here before the ceiling caves in."

He took her hand, his grip strong despite his injury. As they made their way out of the lab, the rift between them seemed smaller, the weight of their shared determination binding them together.

For Eliza, it wasn't just about the mission anymore. It was about the people who stood beside her—especially Marcus. And she wasn't going to let them down.

The roar of flames consumed the lab behind them, the acrid smoke clinging to the night air as Eliza and Marcus stumbled into the alley. Eliza's pulse thundered in her ears, every breath sharp and raw in her chest. Marcus leaned heavily on her shoulder, his weight a reminder of the injury he had taken to save her.

"This way," she said, her voice strained but urgent. Her eyes darted between the shadows ahead and the distant sound of sirens. Whoever had attacked the lab was gone, but she couldn't shake the feeling they were still being watched.

Marcus grunted, each step a battle against the pain in his side. "You sure you know where we're going?"

"Safe house," she replied. "Anna Vega set it up. We'll be secure there—for now."

"Vega," he muttered, his tone laced with skepticism. "Great. Because what we need is a journalist sniffing around for a headline."

"She's more than that," Eliza said sharply, adjusting her grip on him as they moved. "She's one of the only people we can trust."

Marcus didn't argue, though his expression made his feelings clear.

The safe house was tucked into a nondescript block of row houses, its exterior blending seamlessly with its surroundings. Eliza punched in the code Vega had given her, and the door clicked open. The space inside was sparse but clean—a narrow living room with a worn couch, a kitchenette, and a single hallway leading to a bathroom and bedroom.

Marcus sank onto the couch with a groan, his hand pressing against the fresh bandages Eliza had wrapped around his side. "Feels like home already," he muttered.

Eliza shot him a glance but didn't respond, her attention snapping to the sound of footsteps approaching.

Anna Vega appeared in the doorway, her sharp features softened only slightly by the dim light. She carried a laptop bag slung over her shoulder and a notepad in one hand.

"You're late," Vega said, her tone brisk as she shut the door behind her.

"We were a little busy getting blown up," Eliza replied, her voice biting.

Vega raised an eyebrow, her gaze flicking to Marcus. "I see that. You okay?"

"Peachy," Marcus said, wincing as he adjusted his position. "What's with the welcoming committee?"

"Calm down," Vega said, crossing the room. "No one followed you. I made sure of it."

Eliza folded her arms, her exhaustion giving way to frustration. "This wasn't just an attack. They knew exactly what to take. They cleared out the evidence—everything."

"And left you alive," Vega said, her tone pointed. "Which means they're not done with you."

Marcus scowled. "That's comforting."

Vega dropped her bag on the table and opened her notepad. "Tell me everything. What did they take? What did you see?"

Eliza hesitated, her eyes narrowing. "This isn't an interview, Anna."

"No," Vega said, her gaze sharp. "But if you want my help, I need the full picture. If the Order is behind this—and we both know they are—I need to know what we're up against."

Eliza glanced at Marcus, whose expression was guarded. She exhaled, sitting on the edge of the couch. "They took the map, the key, and the residue samples. Everything that could tie the murders to the Order."

"And the lab?" Vega asked.

"Destroyed," Eliza said flatly. "They left nothing but their symbol—carved into my workstation."

Vega tapped her pen against the notepad, her mind clearly racing. "They're not just covering their tracks. They're escalating. Making it personal."

"Tell us something we don't know," Marcus said, his voice dry.

Vega ignored him, leaning forward. "What's the next move?"

Eliza hesitated, her mind a storm of possibilities. "The map pointed to an archive in the Old Quarter—an underground vault tied to the Order. If it's still there, it could have the answers we need."

"Or it could be a trap," Marcus said, his tone sharp.

"Probably," Eliza admitted.

Vega's eyes lit up with curiosity. "And you're going anyway?"

"Yes," Eliza said firmly. "We don't have a choice."

Vega scribbled something in her notepad before looking up. "If you find anything down there, I want to know about it. This could be the story of the century."

"It's not a story," Eliza said, her voice hard. "It's a fight. And if we lose, it's not just us—it's this entire city."

The room fell silent, Vega's expression sobering. "Fair enough," she said quietly. "But you're going to need backup. More than just him." She nodded toward Marcus.

"Hey," Marcus said, his voice laced with mock offense.

Eliza stood, her resolve hardening. "We'll handle it. But right now, we need rest."

Vega nodded, closing her notepad. "Fine. But remember, Eliza—if you don't tell the story, someone else will. And they won't get it right."

Eliza didn't respond as Vega slipped out the door, leaving her and Marcus alone in the quiet safe house.

"You trust her?" Marcus asked, his voice low.

"As much as I trust anyone," Eliza said, sitting beside him.

He shook his head, a faint smile tugging at his lips. "That's not saying much."

"No," she said, her own lips twitching into a faint smile. "It's not."

But even as the tension eased between them, the weight of what lay ahead pressed heavily on Eliza's shoulders. The Order had escalated their game, and she was running out of time to catch up.

The safe house was quiet now, the kind of silence that felt both a relief and a burden. Marcus rested on the worn couch, his head tilted back, his eyes half-closed. The bandages on his side were freshly changed, and the lines of pain on his face had softened, though they hadn't disappeared entirely.

Eliza sat in the armchair across from him, her elbows resting on her knees and her hands clasped tightly. The glow of the single lamp in the room cast long shadows, making the space feel smaller, more intimate. She had barely spoken since Anna Vega had left, her mind a storm of guilt and second-guessing.

Marcus cracked one eye open, his voice breaking the quiet. "You're going to wear a hole in the floor if you keep staring at it like that."

Her lips pressed into a thin line. "I wasn't staring."

"You were," he said with a faint smile. "It's your thinking face. I've seen it enough to know."

She looked up at him, her expression conflicted. "You shouldn't have been there."

He frowned, shifting slightly. "What's that supposed to mean?"

"It means you shouldn't have been the one getting hurt," she said, her voice sharp with self-reproach. "I dragged you into this, Marcus. And now—"

"Now what?" he interrupted, his tone firm. "You're going to sit there and blame yourself for something I chose to do?"

"You didn't choose to get shot!" she snapped, standing abruptly. She paced to the edge of the room, her hands running through her hair. "You didn't sign up for this—none of this was supposed to happen to you."

Marcus watched her, his expression softening despite the tension in her voice. "Eliza, listen to me."

She stopped, her back to him, her shoulders tight.

"I'm here because I want to be," he said. "Because I believe in what you're doing, even if it's dangerous. Especially because it's dangerous. I'm not some helpless bystander—you know that."

She turned slowly, her arms crossed over her chest. "And what happens next time? What happens if I can't protect you?"

He raised an eyebrow. "Protect me? That's rich, coming from the person who runs headfirst into danger every time there's a lead."

"This isn't about me," she said, her voice quieter now.

"Isn't it?" he asked. "Because it seems like you've got this idea in your head that you're responsible for everyone else, that if something goes wrong, it's automatically your fault. Newsflash, Eliza: I'm a grown man. I make my own choices."

Her jaw tightened, but she didn't argue.

"And you know what else?" he continued, his tone softening. "I'm not going anywhere. You can push, you can guilt yourself all you want, but I'm still here. So stop acting like you're carrying this weight alone."

She sank back into the armchair, her arms falling to her sides. "You make it sound so easy."

"It's not," he admitted. "But you don't have to make it harder than it already is."

For a moment, the only sound was the faint hum of the refrigerator in the kitchenette.

"I hate this," she said finally, her voice barely above a whisper.

"Hate what?"

"Putting you in danger," she said, meeting his gaze. "Putting everyone in danger. It's like every time I get close to finding the truth, someone pays the price for it."

He leaned forward slightly, wincing as the movement pulled at his side. "Eliza, this isn't on you. The Order, Cipher—they're the ones pulling the strings. They're the ones hurting people. You're just trying to stop them."

"And what if I can't?" she asked, her voice cracking.

"Then we try again," he said simply.

Her lips quirked into a faint, tired smile. "You make it sound so noble."

"It's not noble," he said, shaking his head. "It's necessary. And you're not doing it alone. Whether you like it or not, you've got me—and I'm not going anywhere."

She looked at him, her eyes softening. "You're impossible, you know that?"

"So I've been told," he said with a grin, though it didn't quite reach his eyes.

The tension in the room eased slightly, though the weight of the moment still lingered.

"You should rest," she said, standing. "We've got a long day ahead of us."

He nodded, leaning back against the couch. "Don't stay up all night brooding, okay?"

"No promises," she said with a faint smile, heading toward the hallway.

As she disappeared into the shadows, Marcus closed his eyes, his breathing evening out. For Eliza, the guilt and fear didn't vanish, but for the first time in days, she felt a sliver of comfort.

She wasn't alone. And for now, that was enough.

Chapter 8
The Order's Web

The air in the hidden archive was damp and heavy, thick with the weight of secrets that had been locked away for decades. Eliza's flashlight carved through the darkness, its beam flickering across shelves stacked with ancient ledgers, faded maps, and sealed boxes bearing the Order's unmistakable sigils. Each step echoed softly, the silence pressing in around her like an unwelcome companion.

Marcus lingered near the entrance, his hand resting on his gun, his eyes scanning the shadows for any sign of trouble. "This place gives me the creeps," he muttered.

"It's not supposed to feel cozy," Eliza replied, her voice low but steady. Her fingers brushed the edge of a worn leather-bound ledger, its pages brittle with age.

"You really think what we need is in here?" he asked, stepping closer to her.

"I don't think," she said, pulling the ledger from the shelf. "I know."

She set the book down on a nearby table, the surface coated with years of dust. The pages were filled with meticulously handwritten records, their ink faded but still legible. Names, dates, transactions—an intricate web of activity that spanned decades.

Marcus peered over her shoulder. "What is this?"

"Documentation," she said, flipping through the pages. "The Order doesn't just operate in the shadows. They keep records of everything—every deal, every bribe, every… participant."

His brow furrowed. "Participants?"

Her hand froze mid-turn, her gaze landing on a familiar name scrawled in the margins of a page. Her stomach dropped, a cold chill sweeping over her.

Malcolm Kain.

"Eliza?" Marcus's voice was cautious now, his eyes narrowing as he caught the change in her expression.

She didn't respond, her fingers tracing the letters of her father's name as though they might vanish under her touch. But the ink didn't fade. The name remained, stark and undeniable, tethered to a list of transactions that detailed bribes and covert operations spanning years.

"This can't be right," she said quietly, her voice barely above a whisper.

Marcus leaned closer, his jaw tightening as he read the entries. "Looks pretty clear to me."

Her breath caught, and she shook her head, turning the page as though the next would somehow prove this one wrong. Instead, she found more evidence—documents outlining meetings, correspondences, and directives. Each one tied her father more deeply to the Order's machinations.

"He told me he walked away," she said, her voice trembling. "That he tried to stop them."

"Maybe he did," Marcus offered, though his tone lacked conviction. "But this doesn't look like someone who walked away."

Her hand hovered over another document, this one stamped with the Order's sigil and marked with her father's signature. "This isn't just involvement," she said, her voice rising with disbelief. "He was part of their leadership."

Marcus placed a hand on her shoulder, steadying her. "Eliza, take a breath. We need to think this through."

She pulled away, pacing the small room, her flashlight beam cutting jagged paths through the darkness. "How could he do this? He stood in front of me and lied—lied about everything. And I believed him. I believed him."

"Eliza," Marcus said firmly, stepping into her path. "This changes things, but it doesn't mean he didn't care about you."

She glared at him, her emotions roiling. "Doesn't mean he didn't care? He's part of the reason this city is drowning in corruption and violence! He's part of the reason people are dead!"

"Maybe," Marcus said, his voice calm but unyielding. "But blowing up now isn't going to help us figure out what to do next."

Her breathing was uneven, her mind a storm of anger and betrayal. She turned back to the table, her hands shaking as she flipped through more pages. Every name, every action documented, felt like another weight pressing down on her.

"What do we do with this?" she asked finally, her voice hollow.

Marcus exhaled, his expression serious. "We use it. This is proof, Eliza—proof of what the Order's done, who they've manipulated, who they've destroyed. And yeah, your dad's on that list. But so are a lot of others."

She clenched her fists, her jaw tight. "I need to confront him."

"Not yet," Marcus said quickly. "You're angry—rightfully so. But if you go after him now, you might not get the answers you need."

She hesitated, her shoulders slumping under the weight of his words. "I don't even know what to ask."

"Start with the truth," he said. "And go from there."

She nodded slowly, her gaze drifting back to the documents. The betrayal she felt was suffocating, but beneath it was a flicker of determination. Her father's lies had brought her here, to this moment, to this truth.

And now, it was her turn to decide what came next.

The air in Malcolm Kain's study was heavy, the scent of aged wood and leather clinging to the room like a memory that refused to fade. The weight of history filled the space, the towering shelves of books and meticulously organized files a silent testament to a lifetime of control and precision. But now, that control was crumbling.

Eliza stood in the center of the room, her fists clenched at her sides, her gaze locked on her father. Malcolm sat behind his desk, his face pale but composed, his hands folded tightly in front of him. The ledger she had found in the archive lay between them, its damning pages open to the entries that bore his name.

"You lied to me," she said, her voice low and trembling with fury.

Malcolm's jaw tightened, his eyes flicking briefly to the ledger before meeting hers again. "Eliza, I—"

"Don't," she snapped, cutting him off. "Don't try to explain it away. Don't tell me you did it for me, or for the city, or for anyone else. I've seen the documents. I've seen what you were part of."

He exhaled slowly, his shoulders sagging. "You don't understand—"

"Then make me understand!" she shouted, slamming her hands down on the desk. "Make me understand how you could be part of something so corrupt, so destructive. Make me understand how you could sit there, pretending to be this moral authority, while you were in bed with them."

Malcolm flinched at her words, his composure cracking. "It wasn't like that," he said, his voice strained.

"Then what was it like?" she demanded. "Because from where I'm standing, it looks pretty damn clear."

He looked away, his hands clenching into fists. "I was young when they approached me. The city was falling apart—crime, corruption, chaos everywhere. The Order offered stability, structure. I thought… I thought I could make a difference from within."

Her laugh was sharp and bitter. "And what difference did you make, Dad? Because all I see are bribes and cover-ups and power plays. All I see are names—names of people who were hurt, or killed, because of the Order. How is that making a difference?"

Malcolm's face crumpled, and for a moment, he looked older, more fragile than she had ever seen him. "I didn't know," he said quietly. "Not at first. I thought I was helping, Eliza. I thought I was keeping the city safe."

"And when you realized what they really were?" she asked, her voice cutting through the silence like a blade.

He hesitated, the weight of his answer dragging him down. "By then, I was too far in. They don't let you walk away, Eliza. You either play along, or you disappear."

Her throat tightened, the anger in her chest burning hotter. "So you played along. You did their dirty work, kept their secrets, all so you could keep your seat on the bench. Don't you dare tell me that was for me."

"It wasn't," he admitted, his voice breaking. "It was for me. I was a coward. I was afraid. And I failed you, Eliza. I failed this city. And I've lived with that failure every single day."

Her breath hitched, the raw emotion in his voice striking a nerve she hadn't expected. But it wasn't enough. It couldn't be enough.

"You don't get to wallow in regret," she said, her voice trembling. "You don't get to sit here and feel sorry for yourself while people are dying because of what you helped create."

He looked up at her, his eyes red-rimmed and glassy. "I never wanted this for you," he said. "I tried to protect you from it, to keep you away from the darkness I let in. But I see now that I only made things worse."

Her hands clenched at her sides, her fury warring with the ache in her chest. "You don't get to make this about protecting me," she said, her voice quieter now but no less sharp. "This was about power. About fear. And now it's about accountability."

Malcolm nodded slowly, his shoulders slumping further. "You're right," he said. "You're right about all of it. I won't ask for your forgiveness, Eliza. I don't deserve it. But if there's anything I can do to help you now—to make this right—I'll do it."

She stared at him, her anger still simmering beneath the surface. "It's too late for that," she said, turning away. "But I'll figure it out. And I'll clean up your mess, because someone has to."

"Eliza—"

She didn't let him finish, walking out of the study without another word. The weight of his confession followed her, but so did the knowledge that the burden of justice was now hers to carry.

And this time, she wouldn't stop until the truth was laid bare.

The sound of Eliza's footsteps echoed through the long hallway outside her father's study, each step heavy with anger, betrayal, and something far more painful—loss. Behind her, Malcolm Kain's voice broke the silence, raw and desperate.

"Eliza! Please, wait!"

She stopped mid-step, her back to him, her fists clenched so tightly her nails bit into her palms. She didn't turn, didn't answer, but the sound of his voice rooted her to the spot.

"Eliza," he called again, louder this time. His footsteps followed hers, uneven and hurried. "I know you're angry. I know you hate me. But please, just… just let me explain—"

She whirled around, her eyes blazing. "Explain? What else is there to explain, Dad? You've done enough!"

Malcolm stopped a few feet from her, his face pale, his eyes filled with anguish. "I haven't," he said quietly. "I haven't done enough—not for you, not for this city. I failed you, Eliza, but I'm trying—"

"Trying?" she interrupted, her voice sharp and trembling. "You're trying now? After all these years, after everything you've done, now you're trying? You don't get to try now!"

"Eliza—"

"No!" she shouted, taking a step closer to him. "Do you know how many nights I spent thinking you were the one person I could trust? That no matter how messed up this city was, no matter how many lies I uncovered, you would be the constant, the one thing that wasn't a lie?"

His shoulders sagged, his hands falling limply to his sides. "I wanted to be that for you," he said softly.

"Then why weren't you?" Her voice cracked, the weight of her words bearing down on her. "Why weren't you, Dad? All I ever needed from you was the truth. Just the truth. But instead, you gave me this—" She gestured wildly, her voice breaking. "A lifetime of lies and excuses!"

Malcolm stepped closer, his voice trembling. "Because I was afraid, Eliza. Afraid of what the truth would do to you. To us. I thought if I could shield you from it—"

"Shield me?" she spat, her voice dripping with bitterness. "You didn't shield me from anything. You just left me to stumble into it, blind and alone. And now—now you want to act like you were doing me a favor?"

"I didn't know how else to protect you!" he shouted, his composure fracturing. "You don't understand what it was like. The choices I had to make—"

"Don't," she snapped, her voice low and dangerous. "Don't you dare try to justify this as a choice. You didn't choose anything for me. You chose for yourself."

His face crumpled, his desperation clear. "You're right," he said, his voice breaking. "I did. I was weak, Eliza. I was selfish. And I would give anything—anything—to go back and fix it."

"But you can't," she said coldly. "You can't undo what you've done, and you can't fix this. You destroyed any chance of that the moment you decided to put yourself before the truth."

Malcolm's lips trembled as he tried to find the words, but none came.

Eliza turned away, her voice softer but no less sharp. "We're done, Dad. Whatever this was—whatever trust I had left—it's gone."

"Don't say that," he said, his voice thick with emotion. "Please, Eliza. Don't walk away from me. I love you. I always have."

She froze, his words cutting through her like a knife. For a moment, she didn't move, her breath caught in her throat.

Finally, she turned her head slightly, just enough for him to see the edge of her profile. "Love isn't enough, Dad. Not anymore."

With that, she walked away, her steps echoing in the stillness. Malcolm stood rooted to the spot, his outstretched hand falling limply to his side as the sound of the door slamming shut rang through the house.

"Eliza!" he called one last time, his voice breaking completely.

But she didn't answer. She didn't stop.

The fracture between them was complete, the bond they had once shared shattered into pieces too jagged to mend. And as Eliza disappeared into the night, the weight of their shared history hung in the air, a wound that neither of them could heal.

The streets were quiet as Eliza walked, the city around her muted under the weight of her thoughts. The events of the night churned in her mind like a relentless tide—the ledger, her father's confession, his desperate pleas as she walked away. The betrayal she felt wasn't just a crack in her world—it was an earthquake that had left nothing standing.

She didn't know how long she had been walking before she found herself at the edge of the city's Old Quarter. The narrow streets and crumbling facades here seemed to mirror her inner turmoil, their history etched into the stone like scars. She stopped beneath a flickering streetlight, the glow casting sharp shadows across her face.

She pulled the ledger fragment from her bag, the paper fragile in her hands. The entries were damning, each one a link in a chain that bound her father to the Order's darkest deeds. But now, that chain felt like her own.

She stared at the document, her jaw tightening. The answers she had spent her life chasing were here, but they came with a cost—a truth that had left her isolated and angry, unsure of who to trust.

But one thing was clear: she couldn't stop now.

Her phone buzzed in her pocket, breaking the silence. She pulled it out, the screen lighting up with Marcus's name. She hesitated, her thumb hovering over the answer button, before letting it go to voicemail.

The silence returned, heavy and suffocating.

"This isn't just about you anymore," she murmured to herself, her voice quiet but resolute.

The words felt foreign, but they were true. This wasn't just about her father or the betrayal that had shattered their relationship. It was about the lives the Order had taken, the power they had stolen, and the city they had left to rot under their control.

She folded the ledger carefully, sliding it back into her bag. Her hand lingered on the strap, her mind racing. Confronting the Order meant stepping into the lion's den—it meant taking on an enemy that thrived in shadows, that had crushed people far more powerful than her without a trace.

And yet, she knew there was no other option.

Her mother's warnings echoed in her mind, faint whispers from a time when Eliza had thought her world was safe and secure. *The Order's roots run deep. Some truths are better left buried.*

But burying the truth wasn't an option anymore. The Order had stolen too much—her family, her trust, her sense of safety. She couldn't let them take anything else.

Her phone buzzed again, a text this time. Marcus.

You okay? Please don't shut me out.

She stared at the message, her chest tightening. Marcus's loyalty had been her anchor, but dragging him any deeper into this felt selfish, reckless. If she was going to face the Order, she needed to do it alone.

Her fingers hovered over the keyboard before she typed back a single message.

I'll be fine. Don't wait up.

She slid the phone into her pocket and turned toward the deeper shadows of the Old Quarter. The map from the archive was burned into her memory, its lines and symbols leading to a forgotten entrance beneath the district. The path forward was clear, even if it was dangerous.

Her steps were deliberate, her resolve hardening with every step. The Order had taken everything from her, but they hadn't broken her. Not yet.

And if this confrontation cost her everything, then so be it.

The city loomed around her, its silence a heavy reminder of what was at stake. But Eliza didn't falter. For the first time in weeks, she felt a grim clarity, a sense of purpose that drowned out the pain and anger.

She would face the Order.

And she would win. Or she would fall trying.

Chapter 9
The Legacy Revealed

The air in the Undercity was heavy, thick with dampness and the metallic tang of rust. The labyrinthine tunnels stretched endlessly, their cracked walls laced with graffiti and forgotten memories. Eliza moved cautiously, her flashlight cutting through the darkness, the faint hum of machinery in the distance guiding her deeper into the heart of the maze.

Her footsteps echoed faintly, the sound swallowed almost immediately by the oppressive silence. Each step felt heavier than the last, not from physical strain but from the growing tension that coiled in her chest. She wasn't alone. She knew that much.

And then she saw him.

Cipher stood in the center of a wide chamber, his silhouette framed by the weak glow of flickering industrial lights. He was tall, his posture relaxed, his hands clasped loosely behind his back. His face was partially obscured by a simple mask, its smooth surface reflecting the light in a way that made him seem both human and otherworldly.

"Dr. Kain," he said, his voice calm and measured, cutting through the silence like a scalpel.

Eliza didn't respond immediately. She stopped several feet away, her flashlight trained on him, her other hand hovering near the holster at her side.

"I was starting to think you wouldn't come," he continued, his tone carrying a faint edge of amusement.

"I'm here," she said, her voice steady despite the storm of emotions roiling inside her.

"Indeed, you are," Cipher replied, tilting his head slightly. "And ahead of schedule. I'm impressed."

"Cut the theatrics," she snapped. "Why did you bring me here? What is this?"

He chuckled softly, a sound that was more unsettling than comforting. "You already know the answer to that, Dr. Kain. You've spent your life chasing the truth, and now you're standing on its threshold."

She took a cautious step closer, her flashlight lowering slightly. "The truth about the Order? About what they've done?"

Cipher nodded slowly. "And about what they are. You see it, don't you? The threads connecting their power, their lies, their violence. They weave a tapestry of control, one you've been unraveling piece by piece."

"I didn't need you to tell me that," she said, her tone sharp.

"No," he agreed. "But you needed me to show you the scale of it. To show you how deep their roots truly run."

Her jaw tightened. "Why? Why do you care? You're just like them—a manipulator, pulling strings from the shadows. How are you any different?"

Cipher's posture remained relaxed, but there was a flicker of something in his tone—amusement, or perhaps condescension. "You misunderstand me. I am not like them. The Order seeks control, stability through domination. I seek freedom—truth, unvarnished and raw. Sometimes, that truth requires chaos to be revealed."

"Chaos," she repeated bitterly. "Is that what you call the murders? The destruction? The lives you've ruined?"

He stepped forward, slowly, his movements deliberate. "Do you know how many lives the Order has destroyed? How many families they've torn apart to preserve their power? What I do is not chaos for its own sake—it's liberation. A scalpel cutting away the cancer they've spread through this city."

"And the people who die in the process?" she demanded, her voice rising. "Are they just collateral damage to you?"

His mask tilted slightly, the reflective surface catching the dim light. "Every revolution requires sacrifice, Dr. Kain. Even you understand that. Or you wouldn't be here."

She hesitated, his words cutting deeper than she wanted to admit. "I didn't come here for a philosophy lesson," she said finally. "If you have something to say, say it."

"I brought you here because you are not like them," he said, his voice softening. "You don't crave power or control. You seek truth, and that makes you dangerous to the Order. But it also makes you valuable—to me."

She narrowed her eyes. "What are you saying?"

"I'm saying," he replied, "that we are on the same path. You see what they are, don't you? The lies they've built their empire upon, the lives they've taken to preserve their illusion of order."

She swallowed hard, her mind racing with the implications of his words. "And what? You think I'll just join you? Become a part of your crusade?"

He chuckled again, the sound low and unsettling. "No, Dr. Kain. I think you already have. The moment you decided to pursue the truth, no matter the cost, you became part of something larger than yourself."

She took a step back, her flashlight rising again. "You don't know me."

"Don't I?" he asked, his tone soft and haunting. "You've seen what they are. You've felt the weight of their lies, the pain of their betrayal. And now, you stand at a crossroads."

The silence between them was heavy, charged with unspoken possibilities.

"What do you want from me?" she asked finally, her voice barely above a whisper.

"To choose," he said simply. "To see the truth for what it is and decide whether you will fight for it—or let the Order bury it forever."

His words hung in the air, their weight pressing down on her. For the first time, Eliza felt the enormity of what lay ahead—not just the danger, but the choices she would have to make, and the sacrifices they would demand.

Cipher stepped back into the shadows, his voice lingering like an echo. "The truth is waiting, Dr. Kain. The question is… are you ready for it?"

And then he was gone, swallowed by the darkness, leaving Eliza alone in the flickering light of the Undercity.

The chamber deep within the Undercity seemed to amplify the tension between them. Cipher stood with an air of calm detachment, his masked face unreadable, while Eliza felt every nerve in her body alight with frustration and unease. The dim, flickering lights above barely pierced the darkness, making the shadows around them feel alive.

"I'll admit," Cipher began, his voice smooth and deliberate, "I wasn't certain you'd come. The truth has a way of scaring people off, even those who claim to seek it."

"I'm not scared of the truth," Eliza shot back, her eyes narrowing. "But I am sick of riddles. You claim to want the same thing I do—justice, accountability—but all I've seen from you is chaos."

Cipher tilted his head slightly, his mask catching the light. "Chaos," he echoed, his tone faintly amused. "A crude word for something far more necessary. Tell me, Dr. Kain, has your so-called lawful justice stopped the Order? Has your painstaking adherence to their rules done anything but strengthen their hold?"

"It's not about their rules," she countered, stepping closer. "It's about holding them accountable, exposing their corruption, and dismantling their power the right way—without becoming like them."

He laughed softly, the sound reverberating through the chamber. "And how is that working out for you? Your evidence stolen, your lab destroyed, your allies endangered. The Order doesn't play by the rules you cling to so desperately, Eliza. They never have."

Her jaw tightened, his words striking too close to the truth. "That doesn't mean I sink to their level," she said, her voice hard. "If I stoop to their methods—if I let destruction and fear become my tools—then I'm no better than they are."

Cipher took a step closer, his posture relaxed but his presence commanding. "You misunderstand me," he said. "I don't destroy for the sake of destruction. I dismantle. I tear apart their foundation brick by brick because that is the only way to ensure it can never be rebuilt."

"And what about the collateral damage?" she snapped. "The people caught in the crossfire? The lives you shatter to make your point?"

"Collateral damage," he repeated, his voice quieter now, almost thoughtful. "An unavoidable cost in any war worth fighting. But consider this, Dr. Kain: how many lives have the Order taken in the shadows, without consequence, without even acknowledgment? How many more will they destroy if you fail?"

Eliza's hands clenched at her sides, her heart pounding. "That doesn't justify what you've done. Murder, manipulation, terror—you've become the very thing you claim to stand against."

"No," Cipher said sharply, his tone cutting through her argument like a blade. "I am what they fear. I don't wear their mask of civility or pretend to work within their broken system. I expose them for what they are and force the world to see."

"And what happens when the dust settles?" she asked, her voice rising. "When you've burned it all to the ground, what's left? Another tyrant to take their place? Another cycle of power and destruction?"

Cipher was silent for a moment, his mask tilted as if he were studying her. "That's where we differ," he said finally. "You believe in the system, in the possibility of redemption for a machine designed to oppress. I don't. I believe in starting over.

In tearing down the rotted structure so something new can grow in its place."

"And you think you're the one to decide that?" she demanded.

"Not alone," he replied. "But someone has to act. Someone has to make the sacrifices you're too afraid to make."

"I'm not afraid," she said, her voice trembling with anger. "I'm willing to sacrifice everything—my safety, my reputation, my relationships—if it means taking them down. But I won't sacrifice innocent lives to do it."

Cipher's head tilted again, as if her words intrigued him. "And that's why you'll lose," he said softly. "Because they'll exploit your restraint. They'll use your morality against you. They always do."

Her breath hitched, his words a dark echo of her own fears. "I don't care," she said after a moment, her voice quieter but no less firm. "I won't become them. If that's what it takes to win, then maybe I don't want to."

Cipher stepped back, his posture as calm as ever. "We'll see," he said simply. "The truth has a way of forcing choices we're not ready to make. And when the time comes, Dr. Kain, I wonder—will you still believe in your system? Or will you see it for the prison it is?"

Eliza stared at him, her chest heaving with suppressed rage and doubt. "I don't need your approval," she said finally. "I'll take the Order down my way. And when I do, I'll make sure everyone knows you're no savior—you're just another manipulator hiding in the shadows."

Cipher chuckled, his voice low and haunting. "Good luck, Dr. Kain. You'll need it."

With that, he turned and disappeared into the darkness, leaving her alone with her thoughts, her doubts, and the weight of the path she had chosen.

The chamber felt colder now, the weight of Cipher's presence lingering even after his figure had retreated back into the shadows. Eliza stood in the faint glow of the overhead lights, her mind whirling with the tension of their exchange. She wasn't sure why she hadn't walked away yet. Maybe it was the faint hope that despite his methods, Cipher's knowledge could be the edge she needed.

The soft scrape of boots on concrete broke her thoughts. Cipher re-emerged from the shadows, this time holding a thin, black folder. He held it out to her, his movements deliberate, almost taunting.

"This," he said, his voice steady, "is everything you need to find the Order's vault."

Eliza hesitated before stepping forward to take the folder. It felt heavier than it should have, the weight of its implications settling over her. She opened it carefully, scanning the contents—a map marked with intricate pathways, coded references to hidden locations, and a list of names she recognized immediately.

"This is real," she murmured, more to herself than to him.

Cipher's masked face gave nothing away, but his voice was laced with quiet triumph. "Of course it is. Unlike the Order, I don't trade in lies."

She looked up at him, her brows furrowed. "Why give this to me? If you had this all along, why not use it yourself?"

"Because it's not about me," he replied, his tone calm but pointed. "I could storm their vault, expose their secrets with a single, well-timed move. But that's not the game we're playing, Dr. Kain. This is about you."

She narrowed her eyes. "What's that supposed to mean?"

"You've spent your life trying to bring them down by their own rules," Cipher said, stepping closer. "But if you want to stop them, you'll need to stop playing their game. You'll need to decide what matters more—principles or victory."

Her grip on the folder tightened. "I can win without becoming like them."

His chuckle was low and humorless. "Can you? The Order thrives because they've mastered the art of manipulation. They've created a system so deeply rooted in fear and control that playing by the rules only reinforces their power. If you want to dismantle them, you'll have to be willing to break the rules."

Eliza shook her head, the tension in her chest coiling tighter. "You don't understand. If I stoop to their level, it's over. Everything I've fought for, everything I believe in—it all becomes meaningless."

"And if you don't?" he countered. "If you keep fighting with one hand tied behind your back, how many more people suffer while you cling to your ideals? How many more lives are lost?"

The words hit harder than she wanted to admit. She thought of the lives the Order had already destroyed—people silenced, families torn apart. She thought of her mother, her death still shrouded in unanswered questions.

Cipher tilted his head, his voice softening. "This isn't about losing yourself, Eliza. It's about understanding that the system they've built isn't just broken—it's a weapon. And weapons aren't dismantled with kind words. They're destroyed."

She looked back at the folder, her heart pounding. "What's in the vault?"

"Everything," Cipher said simply. "Their records, their deals, their leverage. Proof of the lives they've ruined, the crimes they've buried. If you expose it, you could cripple them. But there's a catch."

"Of course there is," she muttered.

He ignored the sarcasm. "The vault is heavily secured. You'll need more than just this map to get in. You'll need to make a choice—a real one."

"What kind of choice?"

Cipher stepped closer, his presence looming. "The kind that forces you to decide what you're willing to sacrifice. The Order doesn't play fair. If you want to win, you'll have to be willing to make hard decisions—decisions you might not come back from."

Her jaw tightened, the weight of his words settling over her. "And if I refuse?"

"Then you've already lost," he said bluntly. "Because the Order counts on people like you—people bound by rules, paralyzed by the fear of crossing a line. They know how to use your morality against you. If you're not willing to bend, they'll break you."

She looked up at him, her eyes blazing. "And you think I should just throw away everything I stand for? Become like them?"

"I think you need to decide what matters more," Cipher said. "Your ideals, or the lives you're trying to save."

The silence between them was thick, the air charged with unspoken tension. Eliza clutched the folder tightly, her mind racing. Cipher's methods repulsed her, but his words forced her to confront a truth she couldn't ignore.

"I'll use this," she said finally, her voice steady but cold. "But don't think for a second that I'm doing it your way."

He stepped back, a faint inclination of his head betraying the faintest trace of approval. "Good. Prove me wrong, Dr. Kain. Show me you can win without becoming like them. But if you falter, if you hesitate, remember this—principles don't stop bullets. And the Order won't show mercy."

With that, he melted back into the shadows, leaving Eliza alone with the folder and the weight of the choice she now faced.

Eliza stared at the map in her hands, the weight of its implications settling over her like a suffocating fog. The routes it displayed were precise, intricate, and laced with danger—just like Cipher himself. Across from her, Cipher stood in the flickering half-light of the Undercity, his masked face unreadable but his presence unnervingly steady.

"You're hesitating," he said, his voice calm, almost amused.

"Of course I'm hesitating," she snapped, lifting her eyes to meet the dark void of his mask. "This isn't just a map. It's a noose. You're asking me to trust you when everything about you screams that I shouldn't."

Cipher tilted his head slightly, the gesture almost mocking. "I'm not asking for trust, Dr. Kain. Trust is a luxury neither of us can afford. I'm offering you a choice—use this to take them down or walk away and leave the Order to tighten its grip."

She clenched her jaw, her fingers tightening around the edges of the map. "And what do you get out of this? You're not doing this out of the kindness of your heart, so what's your angle?"

"I told you already," he said, taking a measured step closer. "I want the same thing you do—to dismantle the Order. To expose them for what they are. You can call it selfish if it helps you sleep at night, but that doesn't change the fact that our goals align."

Eliza studied him, her mind racing. "You make it sound so simple. But nothing about this is simple. You've killed people. You've caused chaos at every turn. And now you expect me to believe you're some kind of martyr for the truth?"

"I expect you to see the bigger picture," he replied smoothly. "Yes, my methods are extreme. Necessary. But what's your alternative? More evidence stolen? More witnesses silenced? You've seen what happens when you play their game by their rules. They win. Every time."

Her stomach twisted at the truth of his words. She hated the way they echoed her own doubts, her own fears about the path she'd been walking. "And what if I take this map, find the vault, and you use it to further your own agenda?"

Cipher chuckled softly, the sound low and humorless. "You're already thinking like them, Dr. Kain. Suspicion, mistrust—it's what the Order thrives on. But let me make this simple: I don't need to manipulate you. You're perfectly capable of finding your way to the truth on your own."

Her brow furrowed as she looked down at the map again. The paths etched onto its surface seemed to pulse with purpose, leading her toward something she couldn't ignore, no matter how much she wanted to.

"What's in the vault?" she asked quietly.

"Leverage," Cipher said. "The kind that can tear their entire operation apart. Names, dates, deals—they've hidden it all there, thinking no one would ever find it."

She looked up sharply. "And you think I'll just hand that over to you when it's done?"

"I think you'll do what you believe is right," he said simply. "That's what makes you dangerous to them—and useful to me."

Her lips pressed into a thin line, her mind churning. The weight of the decision loomed before her like the yawning chasm of the Undercity itself. Trusting Cipher felt like standing on the edge of a knife, but ignoring him meant forfeiting the one clear lead she had to take the Order down.

"You're playing me," she said finally, her voice low.

"I'm giving you a weapon," he corrected. "How you choose to use it is entirely up to you."

The silence between them stretched, thick with tension and unspoken truths. Finally, Eliza folded the map and tucked it into her bag.

"I'll use this," she said, her voice hard but resolute. "But don't mistake this for trust. The second I think you're using me, this uneasy partnership ends."

Cipher inclined his head slightly, the gesture carrying a faint air of triumph. "Fair enough. Just remember, Dr. Kain, the Order doesn't leave loose ends. If you hesitate, they will erase you—and anyone you care about."

Her chest tightened at his words, but she refused to let him see her falter. "I'm not afraid of them," she said coldly.

"Good," he replied, stepping back into the shadows. "Because fear is what they count on."

And with that, he was gone, his presence lingering like a phantom in the air. Eliza stood alone in the dim chamber, the map in her bag and a grim determination settling over her.

She didn't trust Cipher. But for now, she would use him—just as he was using her.

Her path was clearer than ever, but it was also darker, more treacherous. And as she turned to leave the Undercity, she couldn't shake the feeling that the fragile alliance she'd just forged might be the most dangerous choice of all.

Chapter 10
The Councilman's Motive

The hidden chamber was dimly lit, the faint glow of old lanterns casting long shadows against the rough stone walls. Eliza and Marcus crouched behind a stack of crates near the entrance, their breathing shallow as they strained to catch every word of the conversation echoing through the space. The air was thick with the scent of damp stone and aged wood, amplifying the oppressive weight of their surroundings.

Two figures stood at the far end of the chamber, their voices low but sharp with urgency. Eliza adjusted the audio enhancer on her glasses, tuning in to their words as Marcus gave her a questioning glance. She nodded, signaling for him to stay silent.

"...the convergence must happen on schedule," one voice said, its tone clipped and authoritative. "There's no room for delay. The legacy depends on it."

Marcus leaned closer, whispering just above a breath. "Convergence? What are they talking about?"

Eliza shook her head, her gaze locked on the figures. She raised a finger to her lips, urging him to keep quiet. The second voice spoke, deeper and laced with unease.

"We're pushing too hard," the figure said. "The councilman's death already brought too much attention. If we misstep again—"

"We won't," the first interrupted, his tone icy. "The councilman was a necessary sacrifice. He jeopardized everything we've worked for."

Marcus's jaw tightened, his hand instinctively moving toward his holstered weapon. Eliza placed a calming hand on his arm, her focus unwavering.

"The legacy cannot be secured without the convergence," the first voice continued. "Do you understand what's at stake?"

"I understand," the second replied, though doubt lingered in his tone. "But the interference has been... problematic. That investigator—Kain. She's—"

"A nuisance," the first voice cut in, his tone dripping with contempt. "But nothing we can't handle. She doesn't understand what she's up against."

Marcus glanced at Eliza, his brow furrowed. She met his gaze, her lips pressing into a thin line. The mention of her name sent a chill down her spine, but she pushed the fear aside. Focus was paramount.

"What if she gets closer?" the second voice pressed. "What if she uncovers the key locations?"

"She won't," the first voice said with cold certainty. "And even if she does, it'll be too late. The convergence is inevitable. The legacy will be ours."

There was a pause, the tension in the air almost tangible. Marcus leaned toward Eliza, his voice a barely audible whisper. "What the hell is 'the convergence'? And why do they care so much about this 'legacy'?"

"I don't know," Eliza whispered back, her mind racing. "But it's big. Big enough to kill for."

The second figure spoke again, his voice quieter, almost hesitant. "And if she continues? If she gets past the others?"

"Then we deal with her," the first voice said, his tone final. "Permanently."

Marcus's eyes widened, and his grip on his weapon tightened. Eliza placed a hand on his shoulder, silently urging him to stay calm. Their cover was precarious, and any noise could give them away.

The first figure shifted, stepping closer to the second. "You're hesitating. Don't. The legacy is everything. Without it, we lose not just our purpose but our future."

"I understand," the second figure said, though his voice wavered. "I just hope this isn't all for nothing."

"It's not," the first snapped. "Now, secure the site. We'll reconvene before the next phase begins."

The two figures moved toward a side exit, their voices fading as they disappeared into the shadows. Eliza and Marcus remained frozen in place, the weight of what they'd heard sinking in.

After a long moment, Marcus exhaled sharply, breaking the silence. "What the hell did we just stumble into?"

"Pieces of a puzzle," Eliza said, her voice tight. "And we're missing too many of them."

He glanced toward the exit where the figures had disappeared. "This 'convergence'—whatever it is—it sounds like they're betting everything on it."

"And they'll do anything to protect it," Eliza added. She adjusted her glasses, replaying snippets of the conversation she had recorded. "We need to figure out what they mean by 'legacy' and why it's tied to the convergence."

Marcus shook his head, his expression grim. "They're not just protecting a secret, Eliza. They're preparing for something big. And we're running out of time to stop it."

Eliza nodded, her resolve hardening. "Then we move fast. They think they're ahead of us, but they're wrong. We'll figure this out. We have to."

Marcus's gaze softened, though the tension in his posture remained. "Just promise me one thing."

"What's that?" she asked, her tone softening slightly.

"Don't make yourself another 'necessary sacrifice,'" he said, his voice serious.

Eliza managed a faint smile, though it didn't reach her eyes. "Not a chance. We do this together."

"Damn right we do," Marcus said, standing and offering her a hand. "Let's get out of here before they circle back."

Eliza took his hand, rising to her feet. As they slipped out of the chamber, the echoes of the Order's chilling words lingered in her mind. The convergence. The legacy. Whatever it was, it was bigger than anything she'd faced before. But she wasn't going to back down. Not now. Not ever.

The flickering light from Marcus's flashlight danced across the room as Eliza sifted through the stack of documents on the rickety table. The air was thick with dust, the papers brittle with age, but what they revealed was startlingly relevant. Each page seemed to unravel a thread of the councilman's involvement, painting a picture of a man entangled in the Order's secrets—and possibly its downfall.

"Eliza," Marcus said, his voice low as he leaned against the table. "Tell me you've found something."

"More than something," she replied, holding up a heavily annotated memo. The words were scrawled in a hurried hand, the ink blotchy as if written in haste. "This… this changes everything."

He stepped closer, shining his flashlight on the page. "What are we looking at?"

"It's a correspondence," she explained, her tone edged with urgency. "Between the councilman and someone inside the Order. It's vague, but look at this—" She pointed to a line near the bottom. "'The corruption cannot continue. The legacy must be secured, but not at the cost of innocent lives.'"

Marcus frowned, his brow furrowing. "That sounds… idealistic. What does it mean?"

"It means he wasn't just a pawn," Eliza said, flipping to another document. "He was actively trying to fight them. He saw what the Order was doing and wanted to stop it."

"And what, he thought he could just take them down from the inside?" Marcus asked, skepticism lacing his tone.

"Maybe not take them down," Eliza replied, her voice softening. "But he wanted to change something. To expose them, maybe."

Marcus let out a low whistle, shaking his head. "Well, that explains why they wanted him dead. You don't cross a group like this and live to tell about it."

Eliza set the documents down, her fingers brushing the edge of the table as she processed the implications. "He was trying to do the right thing. And they silenced him for it."

Marcus's gaze lingered on her, his expression unreadable. "And now you're in the same position."

She froze, his words cutting through her thoughts. "What are you talking about?"

"I'm talking about you," Marcus said, stepping closer. "You're digging into the same secrets that got the councilman killed. You don't think they're watching? That they don't have plans to deal with you the same way?"

Eliza straightened, her jaw tightening. "This isn't the same."

"Isn't it?" he challenged, his tone sharper than usual. "You're uncovering things no one's supposed to know. You're putting yourself right in their crosshairs."

"That's different," she said, though the conviction in her voice wavered. "I know what I'm doing."

"Do you?" Marcus pressed. "Because from where I'm standing, it looks like you're walking the same path as the councilman. And we both know where that led him."

Eliza's lips parted to respond, but the words caught in her throat. She glanced down at the memo in her hands, the weight of the councilman's final stand pressing heavily on her shoulders. He had tried to make a difference—and paid the ultimate price. Was she doing the same?

"I have to do this," she said finally, her voice quieter now. "If I stop, they win. They get to keep doing this to people. To anyone who gets in their way."

Marcus sighed, dragging a hand through his hair. "I'm not saying stop. I'm saying be careful. You're not just poking the bear, Eliza. You're stealing its damn cubs."

She smirked faintly, though the tension in her shoulders didn't ease. "Then it's a good thing I know how to run."

"This isn't funny," he said, his tone softening. "I'm serious, Eliza. You can't fight them if you're dead."

"I'm not planning on dying," she said firmly, looking up at him. "But I'm not planning on giving up either."

They locked eyes for a moment, the weight of unspoken fears settling between them. Finally, Marcus broke the silence with a sigh.

"Fine," he said, gesturing to the documents. "So, what do these papers tell us? Besides the fact that the councilman had a death wish."

Eliza flipped through the pages again, her focus sharpening. "They show us his plan. He wasn't working alone—he had contacts, allies inside the Order. If we can figure out who they were, we might have a way to stop this."

Marcus arched a brow. "And you think those allies are still alive? After what happened to him?"

"It's possible," she said, though doubt flickered in her voice. "And if they are, they might be able to tell us what 'the legacy' and 'the convergence' actually mean."

Marcus shook his head, his skepticism clear. "You're banking on a lot of 'ifs,' Eliza."

"I don't have a choice," she said, her voice hardening. "This is the best lead we've got."

He studied her for a moment before nodding reluctantly. "Then let's make it count. But you're not doing this alone."

"I never planned to," she replied with a faint smile.

"Good," Marcus said, turning toward the exit. "Because someone's got to keep you alive long enough to finish this."

As they gathered the documents and left the chamber, Eliza felt the weight of the councilman's legacy pressing on her. His fight wasn't over—and now, it was hers.

The chamber's dim light felt heavier now, its shadows clinging to the walls as Eliza sifted through another stack of papers. Her glasses glowed faintly as they scanned documents, cross-referencing names and locations against her growing mental map of the Order's activities. Each new piece of information deepened the knot in her stomach. This wasn't just about the councilman or the Order's secrecy—it was something far bigger.

"Eliza," Marcus called from the other side of the room. His voice was taut, his frustration barely concealed. "We've been here too long. We need to move."

"Just a minute," she replied, her tone distracted as she scanned another page. "There's something here. I can feel it."

He sighed audibly, walking over to her. "You've been saying that for the last twenty minutes. Meanwhile, we're sitting ducks. If they come back—"

"Then we'll deal with it," Eliza interrupted, her eyes never leaving the paper in her hands. "Look at this." She held it out to him, her voice edged with urgency.

Marcus took the paper reluctantly, his brow furrowing as he skimmed the contents. "Another logistics report? What am I looking at?"

"It's not just logistics," she said, pointing to a line of coded entries. "These aren't transport routes—they're deployment zones. Look at the dates. These are coordinated actions."

Marcus's expression darkened as he handed the paper back. "Coordinated actions for what?"

"That's what I'm trying to figure out," Eliza admitted, her fingers brushing against a map pinned beneath the stack of documents. She unfolded it carefully, revealing a detailed layout of the city. Marked across it were several key locations—government buildings, infrastructure hubs, and residential zones.

"Okay, this is getting ridiculous," Marcus said, stepping back to take it all in. "Why would they care about half of these places? And why mark them so carefully?"

"Because it's not just about secrecy," Eliza said, her voice low but firm. "This isn't just about protecting their operations. They're planning something. Something bigger."

Marcus crossed his arms, his expression skeptical. "And you're basing that on a few maps and cryptic notes?"

"I'm basing it on everything we've seen," she countered, meeting his gaze. "The councilman's warnings, the way they've escalated their threats, the resources they're pouring into this. They're not just hiding—they're preparing."

"For what?" Marcus pressed, his tone rising. "You keep saying they're 'planning something,' but what does that even mean? A takeover? A terrorist attack? What?"

"I don't know yet," Eliza admitted, her voice softening slightly. "But if we can figure out what 'the convergence' is, we'll have our answer."

Marcus ran a hand through his hair, exhaling sharply. "You're guessing, Eliza. You're piecing together scraps and jumping to conclusions."

"That's how investigations work," she snapped, her frustration breaking through. "You follow the scraps until they lead you to the truth."

"And what happens when those scraps get us killed?" Marcus shot back. "Because that's where this is heading."

She turned away, her gaze falling back to the map. "If we walk away now, we'll never know what they're planning. We'll never stop them."

Marcus stepped closer, his voice softer but no less firm. "Maybe we can't stop them. Not alone."

Eliza looked at him sharply. "What are you saying?"

"I'm saying we need help," he replied. "This is bigger than us. If they're planning something citywide, we need to bring in someone who can actually do something about it."

"And who would that be?" she challenged, her voice rising. "The police? The government? You think they'd believe us? Or worse—you think they're not already involved?"

Marcus hesitated, his jaw tightening. "You don't know that."

"And you don't know they're not," Eliza said, stepping closer to him. "The Order has been operating in the shadows for decades. You really think they don't have people on the inside?"

He sighed, shaking his head. "So, what's your plan? Keep going until we're out of leads or out of luck?"

"No," she said firmly. "We keep going until we figure out what they're doing and how to stop it. We're already in this, Marcus. There's no turning back now."

He stared at her for a long moment, his frustration giving way to reluctant resolve. "You're impossible."

"And you're stubborn," she shot back with a faint smirk. "That's why we make a good team."

Marcus chuckled despite himself, though the tension in his shoulders didn't ease. "Fine. But if we're doing this your way, we're doing it smart. No more solo missions, no more reckless stunts."

"Deal," Eliza said, her smirk fading as she looked back at the map. The marked locations seemed to taunt her, each one a piece of a puzzle she couldn't yet see clearly. "Whatever this is, it's bigger than we thought."

"And more dangerous," Marcus added.

She nodded, her resolve hardening. "But that's never stopped us before."

He sighed again, gesturing toward the exit. "Let's get out of here before we push our luck. We can figure out our next move somewhere less… incriminating."

As they left the chamber, the weight of the Order's plans pressed heavily on Eliza's mind. Whatever the "convergence" was, she knew it would change everything. And she was determined to stop it—no matter the cost.

The air in the chamber was still as Eliza carefully folded the stolen documents, slipping them into her bag. Marcus stood near the entrance, his flashlight off, his stance tense. His ears strained for the faintest sound beyond the stone doorway. The weight of their discovery was palpable, but the uneasy silence made it hard to savor the victory.

"Eliza," Marcus said in a whisper, barely loud enough to break the silence. "We need to move. Now."

"Just one more," Eliza murmured, rifling through another set of papers spread across the table. Her hands worked quickly, the urgency in her movements barely masking her determination. "If we leave without this—"

"Forget it," Marcus hissed, cutting her off. "They're coming. I heard something."

She froze, glancing at him sharply. "Are you sure?"

The sound of muffled voices drifted faintly down the hallway, the words indistinct but growing louder. Marcus gave her a pointed look, his hand moving instinctively to his holstered weapon. "Does that answer your question?"

Eliza didn't argue. She stuffed the last document into her bag, zipped it shut, and slung it over her shoulder. Marcus gestured for her to follow, and they moved toward the opposite side of the chamber, keeping to the shadows. The stone walls felt cold and rough against their backs as they pressed against them, listening.

The voices grew clearer, the unmistakable cadence of two men deep in conversation. Eliza's breath hitched as she caught fragments of their words.

"...can't let this delay us," one voice said, firm and commanding. "The convergence takes priority."

"The security breach," another voice replied, lower and gruff. "If they've already accessed this site—"

"They won't get far," the first voice interrupted. "We'll find them."

Eliza glanced at Marcus, her expression tense. He leaned closer, his voice barely audible. "We're running out of time."

"Not yet," Eliza whispered back, her gaze darting to a narrow passageway on the far side of the chamber. "There's another exit."

"And it's probably rigged," Marcus muttered, his frustration evident.

"It's our only shot," she said. "Unless you want to introduce yourself to them."

He glared at her but didn't argue. Together, they edged toward the passageway, their steps slow and deliberate. The faint flicker of light from the Order members' lanterns grew brighter, casting long shadows into the chamber.

As they reached the passageway, Marcus paused, turning to Eliza. "I'll go first. Stay close, and for the love of God, don't make a sound."

Eliza nodded, her heart pounding as she followed him into the narrow corridor. The walls seemed to close in around them, the air growing colder with every step. Behind them, the voices continued, punctuated by the occasional scrape of boots against stone.

"We shouldn't be here," Marcus muttered under his breath as they navigated the twisting path. "This whole thing feels like a trap."

"We're past that point," Eliza replied, her voice barely above a whisper. "Just keep moving."

The passageway twisted sharply, opening into a smaller chamber filled with discarded crates and broken machinery. Marcus motioned for her to stop, his eyes scanning the room for any sign of danger.

"Clear," he said after a moment, though his voice lacked conviction. "Let's move."

As they crossed the room, the sound of the Order members grew louder. Eliza glanced over her shoulder, her chest tightening as a faint glow from their lanterns illuminated the far end of the passageway.

"They're close," she whispered, quickening her pace.

"No kidding," Marcus replied, his tone sharp. "Find the exit."

Eliza's glasses scanned the room, highlighting a faint draft near a collapsed section of the wall. She pointed to it. "There. It's hidden, but it leads outside."

"Let's hope you're right," Marcus said, already moving toward it.

They squeezed through the narrow gap, emerging into the cool night air. The sky was a deep indigo, the stars obscured by clouds. Eliza took a deep breath, her chest heaving as she adjusted her bag.

"We're clear," Marcus said, glancing around. "For now."

"Not for long," Eliza replied, her voice tense. "They'll realize we were here."

"Then we'd better make this count," he said, his tone hardening. "What's the plan?"

Eliza pulled out one of the stolen documents, her eyes scanning the coded text. "We decode this. We figure out what 'the convergence' really means."

"And if it's worse than we think?" Marcus asked, his voice softer now.

"Then we stop it," she said firmly, meeting his gaze. "No matter what it takes."

He sighed, shaking his head. "You're relentless. You know that?"

"It's what keeps us alive," Eliza replied, a faint smirk breaking through her resolve.

Marcus chuckled despite himself, though the tension in his shoulders didn't ease. "Let's hope you're right."

Together, they disappeared into the shadows, the stolen evidence clutched tightly in their hands. The Order's plans were beginning to unravel, and Eliza was determined to see them exposed—even if it meant risking everything.

Chapter 11
A Mother's Warning

The dim light of the safehouse cast long shadows across the small desk where Eliza sat, her mother's journal spread open before her. The leather-bound book was worn, its edges frayed from years of handling. Each page was a testament to her mother's relentless pursuit of knowledge—filled with sketches, notes, and cryptic annotations that felt both familiar and alien.

Eliza's fingers trailed over the faded ink of a detailed symbol, its intricate lines matching the ones she had seen carved into the walls of the tunnels. Her mother's precise handwriting looped around the sketch, the words hinting at something far more sinister than Eliza had ever imagined.

"The convergence," she murmured, her voice barely above a whisper. The word appeared multiple times across the pages, always accompanied by phrases like *"synchronization of forces"* and *"a necessary alignment."*

"What did you find?" Marcus's voice broke through her concentration, pulling her gaze from the journal. He stood in the doorway, his expression a mix of curiosity and concern.

Eliza looked up, her brow furrowed. "My mother knew about the Order. She wasn't just studying symbols—she was tracking their activities. Look at this."

She turned the journal toward him, pointing to a passage written in bold, urgent strokes: *"The experiments are escalating. The convergence will come at a cost too great to bear."*

Marcus stepped closer, his eyes scanning the page. "Experiments? What kind of experiments?"

Eliza shook her head, frustration tightening her chest. "She doesn't say, at least not directly. But these symbols—" she tapped another sketch, a pattern that matched one she had seen glowing in the tunnels. "They're not just decorative. They're part of something. A process. Maybe even a ritual."

Marcus leaned against the desk, crossing his arms. "And she connected these to the Order? To their... 'legacy,' or whatever they call it?"

"She must have," Eliza said, flipping through the pages. Her mother's handwriting shifted in tone as the journal progressed—starting methodical, almost clinical, but growing more frantic with every entry. "Look here."

She pointed to a newer section, the ink darker and less steady: *"The synchronization will tear the city apart. I have to stop this before they succeed."*

Marcus frowned, his expression darkening. "She was trying to stop them?"

Eliza nodded, her throat tightening. "It sounds like she uncovered something huge. But she didn't have enough time to piece it all together. Or to stop them."

He exhaled, his hand running through his hair. "And now it's on you."

"It always was," Eliza replied softly. She flipped to another page, this one containing a list of coordinates and dates. Beside each was a single word: *"Event."*

"What do these mean?" Marcus asked, pointing to the list.

"I don't know yet," Eliza admitted, her voice edged with frustration. "But these dates… they're all from years ago. And the locations match sites we've already linked to the Order. This isn't random."

"None of this is," Marcus said, stepping back. "But experiments? Rituals? Convergence? It sounds like we're dealing with something way beyond our pay grade."

Eliza met his gaze, her resolve hardening. "Then we elevate our game. My mother didn't back down, and neither will I."

"Your mom didn't have backup," Marcus countered, his tone softening. "She didn't have anyone to pull her out when things went sideways. You do."

Eliza smiled faintly, though it didn't reach her eyes. "And I'm grateful for that. But this… this is personal. Whatever the Order is planning, it's connected to her death. I need to see this through."

"And I'll be right there with you," Marcus said, his voice steady. "But let's not rush into anything blind. We need to figure out exactly what these experiments were—and what your mother knew—before we make our next move."

Eliza nodded, returning her attention to the journal. Her fingers brushed over the final pages, the ink lighter here, as if her mother had written in haste. One entry stood out, its words simple but chilling:

"The convergence is not what it seems. The legacy is not worth the cost. They will silence anyone who gets too close. Stay vigilant. Stay alive."

Her chest tightened, the weight of her mother's warning sinking in. "She knew they'd come after her."

"And now they're coming after you," Marcus said grimly.

Eliza closed the journal, her hands shaking slightly. "Then we need to finish what she started. Before it's too late."

The room fell into a heavy silence, broken only by the faint hum of the safehouse's heater. Eliza's determination burned brighter than ever, but so did the fear lurking in the corners of her mind. Whatever the convergence was, it was bigger than she had imagined. And she was running out of time to stop it.

Eliza sat cross-legged on the floor of the safehouse, surrounded by an assortment of maps, notes, and photographs spread out like the pieces of an unsolvable puzzle. Her mother's journal rested in her lap, its pages open to the section filled with coordinates and hastily scrawled warnings. A cold cup of coffee sat forgotten on the table beside her as her mind worked to untangle the threads her mother had left behind.

"This doesn't add up," she muttered, tapping a pen against her knee. "The dates, the locations… something's missing."

Marcus leaned against the doorframe, watching her with a mix of concern and curiosity. "You've been at this for hours," he said, crossing his arms. "Maybe it's time to take a step back."

"I can't," she replied without looking up. "There's a connection here. I just can't see it yet."

Marcus sighed and stepped closer, crouching beside her. He picked up one of the maps, his brow furrowing as he scanned the red circles Eliza had drawn around certain locations. "All right," he said. "Walk me through it. What are we looking at?"

"These," Eliza said, pointing to the circles on the map, "are sites where we know the Order has been active. Tunnels, factories, abandoned buildings… all linked to their operations."

"And these?" Marcus gestured to the list of dates and coordinates from the journal.

"They match some of the sites, but not all," she said, flipping through the pages. "It's like my mother was tracking something bigger than just their movements. Something coordinated."

"Coordinated how?" Marcus asked, his tone skeptical. "You think this 'convergence' ties it all together?"

"I know it does," Eliza said, her voice sharpening. "The Order's not just protecting their secrets—they're building toward something. My mother saw it, but she didn't live long enough to figure out what."

Marcus ran a hand through his hair, exhaling sharply. "And now you're supposed to pick up where she left off. No pressure, right?"

Eliza shot him a look. "If you're not going to help, don't distract me."

"I'm helping," he said, holding up his hands. "I just don't want you to burn out before we get anywhere."

She sighed, softening slightly. "Sorry. It's just... this is bigger than I thought. Bigger than she thought. And if we don't stop them—"

"I get it," Marcus interrupted, his voice steady. "But running yourself into the ground isn't going to help anyone."

Eliza hesitated, then nodded. "Okay. Let's focus on what we know." She pulled a photograph from the pile and handed it to him. "This was taken near one of the marked locations. Look at the symbols on the crates."

Marcus studied the photo, his eyes narrowing. "Same as the ones in the tunnels. So they were moving something."

"Exactly," Eliza said. "And not just to one place. They were transporting materials to multiple sites, all leading up to something. The convergence."

Marcus set the photo down and leaned forward, scanning the notes scattered around them. "And you think these locations are part of it?"

"They have to be," Eliza said, flipping to another page in the journal. "Look at this entry. My mother wrote about a pattern—a sequence of events tied to specific dates and places. It's like they're synchronizing something."

"Synchronizing what?" Marcus asked, his skepticism returning. "You keep saying this, but you still don't know what they're planning."

"I'm getting closer," Eliza said, her voice resolute. "If I can decode her notes, I'll figure out what they're after. And why they killed her to keep it hidden."

Marcus was silent for a moment, his gaze shifting between her and the scattered evidence. "You're sure about this?" he asked quietly.

"More than I've ever been," she replied. "This is bigger than her death, Marcus. It's about the entire city. Maybe more."

He let out a low whistle, leaning back on his heels. "All right. What's our next move?"

Eliza gestured to the maps and journal. "We cross-reference everything. Find the locations that overlap with the most recent Order activity. If we can pinpoint their next move, we might be able to stop them before the convergence happens."

Marcus nodded, a faint smirk tugging at his lips. "You know, you're kind of terrifying when you get like this."

"Good," Eliza said with a faint smile. "I'll need you to keep up."

He chuckled, shaking his head. "Don't worry about me. Just don't forget to eat or sleep while you're saving the world, all right?"

"I'll try," she said, her smile fading as her focus returned to the map. The weight of her mother's legacy pressed heavily on her shoulders, but she refused to falter. The pieces were coming together, slowly but surely, and she was determined to finish what her mother had started—no matter the cost.

The room was quiet except for the soft rustle of papers as Eliza sifted through the contents of her mother's journal. A folded piece of paper, tucked between the last few pages, caught her attention. Its edges were yellowed, the creases worn, as though it had been opened and closed countless times. Her pulse quickened as she carefully unfolded it, revealing her mother's unmistakable handwriting.

"Eliza, what is it?" Marcus asked, noticing the change in her demeanor.

"A letter," she murmured, her eyes scanning the first few lines. Her breath hitched, and she tightened her grip on the paper. "It's from her. From my mother."

Marcus stepped closer, leaning against the edge of the table. "What does it say?"

Eliza hesitated, her voice trembling as she began to read aloud. "'Eliza, if you're reading this, it means I'm no longer with you.'" She paused, swallowing hard before continuing. "'There are things I wanted to tell you, things I should have told you long ago. But I thought I had more time.'"

"Eliza," Marcus said softly, his voice laced with concern. "You don't have to—"

"I need to," she interrupted, her gaze fixed on the letter. She took a steadying breath and read on. "'The Concordant Order is dangerous, more dangerous than I ever realized when I first began my research. They are not just a group protecting secrets—they are the architects of something that could change everything. And not for the better.'"

Marcus let out a low whistle, his arms crossing over his chest. "She knew about all of this? The experiments, the convergence?"

"It sounds like it," Eliza said, her voice tight. She continued reading. "'I wanted to shield you from this world, but I see now that I was wrong. If you've found this letter, it means you're already involved. And if that's the case, then you must be careful.'" She paused, her voice trembling slightly. "'Promise me, Eliza, that you will not let them consume you. Do not let their lies cloud your judgment.'"

Marcus shook his head, his jaw tightening. "She wanted to protect you. She didn't want you to follow her path."

Eliza looked up at him, her eyes fierce. "She also wanted me to know the truth." She glanced back at the letter. "'Find the truth,'" she read aloud, her voice gaining strength. "'It's the only way to stop them. But you must do so with caution. They will stop at nothing to silence anyone who gets too close. I hope you never have to face them, but if you do, remember this: You are stronger than they think. And you are not alone.'"

Marcus shifted uncomfortably, his gaze fixed on the letter. "She sounds like she knew exactly what you'd end up doing."

"Maybe she did," Eliza said quietly, folding the letter and placing it carefully back in the journal. She sat back, her mind racing with questions and emotions she couldn't yet untangle.

"You okay?" Marcus asked, his voice softer now.

"I don't know," she admitted, looking down at her hands. "I spent so long trying to understand her work, trying to figure out why she kept it all a secret. And now…" She trailed off, shaking her head. "Now I see she was trying to protect me."

"And herself," Marcus added. "She knew what she was up against. She knew how dangerous they are."

Eliza looked at him, her expression resolute. "But she also believed in finding the truth. She didn't want me to give up."

"No," Marcus said, meeting her gaze. "But she didn't want you to die for it either."

"That's not going to happen," Eliza said firmly. "I'm going to finish this. For her. For all the people they've hurt."

Marcus sighed, running a hand through his hair. "You're relentless, you know that?"

"She taught me well," Eliza replied with a faint smile. She picked up the journal and tucked the letter safely back inside. "Come on. We have work to do."

As she stood, Marcus reached out, his hand brushing her arm. "Eliza," he said, his voice steady but serious. "Promise me you'll be careful. Whatever we're walking into, I need to know you won't take unnecessary risks."

She looked at him for a long moment before nodding. "I promise. But I'm not stopping, Marcus. Not until we end this."

He gave her a faint smile, his hand dropping back to his side. "That's all I needed to hear."

Together, they turned back to the maps and notes spread across the table. The truth her mother had pursued was finally within reach, and Eliza was more determined than ever to uncover it—even if it meant facing the same danger her mother had tried so desperately to warn her about.

The air in the safehouse felt heavier as Eliza stood by the desk, staring down at her mother's journal. The letter she had read moments earlier weighed heavily on her mind, each word etched into her memory like a brand. Her mother's warnings had been clear, but so had her encouragement—find the truth. It was both a caution and a call to action.

Eliza's hand rested on the journal's cover, her fingers tracing the worn leather. "She knew this was coming," she said softly, her voice breaking the silence. "She knew I'd end up here."

Marcus stood a few feet away, leaning against the wall. His arms were crossed, his expression unreadable. "Maybe she did," he said finally. "But I'm guessing she didn't want this for you."

Eliza looked up at him, her eyes sharp. "No, she didn't. But that doesn't matter now. I'm already in it. And if I walk away, everything she worked for—everything she gave her life for—will mean nothing."

Marcus sighed, pushing off the wall and stepping closer. "No one's saying walk away. I'm just saying… be smart about it. You're not your mother, Eliza."

"I know," she said, her tone firm. "But that's exactly why I have to do this. She started something, and it's up to me to finish it. No one else can."

Marcus nodded slowly, his gaze shifting to the journal. "So, what's next? You've got her notes, her warnings. What do we do with it?"

Eliza opened the journal again, flipping through the pages with newfound purpose. Each entry, every cryptic note, seemed to carry more weight now, her mother's voice guiding her through the chaos. She stopped at a sketch of a symbol, one she had seen carved into the walls of the tunnels. Her mother's handwriting surrounded it, detailing connections to places and people Eliza hadn't fully pieced together yet.

"This," she said, pointing to the symbol. "This is the key. It's everywhere—in the tunnels, in the documents we found, even in the locations my mother marked. It's all tied to the convergence."

"And the convergence is tied to the legacy," Marcus added, stepping beside her. "Whatever that means."

"It means they're planning something big," Eliza said, her voice hardening. "Something that involves the city, maybe even more. And they'll do anything to keep it a secret."

Marcus studied her for a moment, his jaw tightening. "You're sure about this? Because once we move forward, there's no going back."

"I was sure the moment I opened that letter," she replied, meeting his gaze. "We have to stop them, Marcus. No one else will."

He exhaled sharply, a faint smirk tugging at the corner of his mouth. "All right, Kain. I'm in. But you're calling the shots. Just don't get us killed."

Eliza smiled faintly, the weight on her chest easing slightly. "I'll do my best."

They worked in silence for a while, organizing the documents and cross-referencing the notes her mother had left behind. The sense of urgency pressed down on Eliza, but so did a renewed clarity. For the first time, the pieces felt like they were coming together.

Marcus broke the silence. "Your mother was brave. Reckless, maybe, but brave."

Eliza paused, looking at him. "She was. And she was right about the Order. They've been in the shadows for too long."

"And now they're going to regret it," Marcus said, his voice tinged with resolve.

Eliza nodded, her expression fierce. "They are. Because this time, they're not the only ones with a plan."

As the night deepened, the safehouse buzzed with activity. Eliza and Marcus prepared for the next steps, their resolve unshakable. Whatever the convergence was, whatever the

Order was planning, they were ready to face it head-on. For her mother. For the truth. For the legacy that was now hers to protect.

Chapter 12
Into the Depths

The faint beam from Eliza's flashlight swept across the jagged walls of the tunnel, the dim light barely cutting through the oppressive darkness. The air was damp and stale, carrying a metallic tang that clung to her senses. Behind her, Marcus followed closely, his steps careful but deliberate. In his hand, he held the stolen map, its edges frayed from their constant reference.

"This way," Marcus said, his voice low as he pointed to the left fork in the path. The map's markings were precise, showing faint lines converging on a central chamber deeper within the maze. "The chamber should be about half a mile ahead, give or take."

Eliza adjusted the strap of her bag, her other hand gripping the flashlight tightly. "Half a mile of what, though? More traps? More symbols? Or something worse?"

Marcus smirked faintly, though his eyes remained sharp. "Probably all of the above. The Order doesn't strike me as the 'leave it unguarded' type."

"Good," Eliza replied, her tone steely. "That means we're on the right track."

The tunnel narrowed as they pressed forward, the walls seeming to close in around them. The faint scuff of their boots echoed off the stone, amplified by the silence that stretched between them. Eliza's mind churned with the implications of their journey, the weight of her mother's warnings sitting heavily on her shoulders.

After a few minutes, Marcus stopped abruptly, holding up a hand. "Wait," he said, crouching down to examine the ground.

"What is it?" Eliza asked, kneeling beside him.

He pointed to the faint outline of a pressure plate, its edges barely visible beneath a thin layer of dirt and dust. "Trap," he said. "Looks mechanical—spring-loaded, maybe. Step on this, and something nasty comes flying at you."

Eliza leaned closer, her forensic glasses scanning the mechanism. "It's definitely mechanical," she said. "Connected to…" She traced a faint wire running along the edge of the wall. "A projectile launcher. Looks like darts or arrows. Lethal."

Marcus straightened, stepping back carefully. "Good thing we're paying attention. Think you can disable it?"

"Of course," Eliza replied, her tone clipped. She pulled a small multi-tool from her bag and carefully began to disarm the device. Her fingers moved deftly, years of training and experience guiding her. After a few tense moments, the wire snapped, and the plate locked in place.

"There," she said, standing and dusting off her hands. "It's safe now."

Marcus gave her an approving nod. "Remind me to always bring you along when I'm navigating death traps."

She smirked faintly. "You'd be lost without me."

As they continued deeper into the tunnel, the air grew heavier, thick with an acrid chemical smell that burned their noses. Eliza stopped, scanning the walls and floor with her glasses.

"Chemical residue," she said, pointing to a faint discoloration on the stone. "It's recent. Probably triggered by proximity."

Marcus frowned, pulling his shirt up over his nose. "What kind of chemicals are we talking about? Poison gas? Acid?"

"Could be either," Eliza replied, her voice tense. "Let's not find out."

She examined the residue more closely, identifying faint lines leading to a small vent embedded in the wall. "There's a dispersal system here. It's dormant now, but if we step into the wrong spot…"

"Got it," Marcus said, carefully stepping around the discolored area. "Avoid the shiny patches. Easy enough."

"Easy until they stop being obvious," Eliza muttered, following his lead.

The tunnel narrowed further, forcing them to move single file. The weight of the stone above them pressed down, the oppressive silence broken only by the occasional drip of water from the ceiling.

"Are we close?" Eliza asked, her voice low.

Marcus glanced at the map, his flashlight illuminating the faded markings. "Should be just ahead," he said. "If this thing is accurate."

"It's accurate," Eliza replied. "The Order wouldn't go through this much trouble if it wasn't leading to something important."

The tunnel suddenly widened, opening into a larger passageway. The air was colder here, and the faint glow of symbols etched into the walls cast an eerie light. Marcus and Eliza exchanged a glance, their unspoken agreement clear—this was the right place.

"Be ready for anything," Marcus said, his hand resting on the grip of his weapon.

"I always am," Eliza replied, her gaze locked on the path ahead.

As they moved closer to the central chamber, the symbols grew more intricate, their patterns twisting and overlapping in ways that made Eliza's head spin. The traps, the chemicals, the symbols—they all pointed to one thing: the Order's determination to protect whatever lay at the heart of this labyrinth.

For Eliza, that only made her more certain. Whatever was in the central chamber, it was worth the risk.

The tunnel abruptly widened into a small antechamber, its walls lined with shelves carved into the stone. Dust coated every surface, and the stale air smelled faintly of mildew and decay. Eliza and Marcus froze at the threshold, their flashlights casting long, eerie shadows across the forgotten room.

"What is this?" Marcus muttered, stepping cautiously inside. His flashlight beam swept across rows of ancient-looking artifacts: weathered scrolls, rusted tools, and tattered books stacked precariously on the shelves.

Eliza followed him, her forensic glasses scanning the room for hidden details. "A storage room," she said, her voice tinged with both awe and urgency. "But not just for artifacts—look at this."

She gestured toward a large wooden table in the center of the chamber. Strewn across its surface were photographs, faded but still legible, and diagrams filled with intricate symbols. Eliza's eyes widened as she recognized some of the patterns etched into the walls of the tunnels.

"Those symbols," she murmured, stepping closer. "They're everywhere—on the walls, the documents, even in the councilman's office. They're part of the Order's language."

Marcus picked up a photograph, his brow furrowing. "This is a political rally," he said, holding it up for her to see. The black-and-white image showed a crowd gathered in front of a podium, with a figure speaking passionately. "It's dated... 1974. Why would the Order care about this?"

Eliza scanned the image with her glasses. Faintly, in the background, she spotted the unmistakable symbol of the Concordant Order etched into the podium's base. "Because they were there," she said. "They've been influencing events for decades—probably longer."

Marcus set the photo down, his jaw tightening. "So, what? They're some shadowy puppet masters pulling strings behind the scenes?"

"Maybe," Eliza replied, flipping through a stack of yellowed papers. Her heart raced as she skimmed notes written in precise, almost clinical handwriting. "Or maybe they're doing more than pulling strings. Look at this."

She handed him a document labeled *Experimental Synchronization Protocols*. The words were cryptic, filled with jargon and references to energy fields and synchronization points. Marcus frowned as he read.

"This sounds... like science fiction," he said, shaking his head. "Synchronization protocols? Energy fields? What the hell does that even mean?"

"It means they're conducting experiments," Eliza said, her voice tight. "And not just small ones. Look at the scale of this."

She spread a large diagram across the table, revealing a detailed map of the city. Key locations were marked with the same symbols they had seen throughout the tunnels. Lines connected the locations in intricate patterns, converging on a single point in the center of the map.

"The central chamber," Eliza whispered, her finger tracing the lines. "Everything leads back here."

Marcus leaned over the map, his expression darkening. "And these experiments? You think they're happening below the city?"

"I don't think," Eliza replied, her voice hardening. "I know. My mother's journal hinted at something like this—large-scale operations, experiments tied to energy synchronization. But I didn't realize how deeply embedded it was."

Marcus let out a low whistle, stepping back from the table. "So, what's their goal? What's the point of all this?"

"That's what we need to figure out," Eliza said, her eyes scanning the rest of the documents. "Whatever it is, it's tied to the convergence. And if we don't stop it—"

"We won't let it get that far," Marcus interrupted, his tone resolute. "But we need more than half-cryptic notes and creepy diagrams. We need solid proof."

Eliza nodded, turning her attention to a stack of photographs near the edge of the table. She flipped through them quickly, her heart pounding as she recognized the councilman in one of the images. He was shaking hands with a man whose face was obscured, but the background showed one of the marked sites on the map.

"They were working together," she said, holding up the photo. "The councilman wasn't just a victim—he was part of this. At least, at some point."

Marcus studied the photo, his jaw tightening. "Then something changed. He found out too much, tried to expose them."

"And they silenced him," Eliza finished, setting the photo down. She took a deep breath, the weight of their discoveries pressing heavily on her. "This isn't just about secrecy, Marcus. The Order isn't protecting something—they're building something. And whatever it is, it's massive."

Marcus gestured to the documents. "Then let's take what we can and get out of here. The longer we stay, the more we're risking."

Eliza hesitated, her gaze lingering on the map. The central chamber loomed in her mind, its purpose still unclear but undeniably important. She nodded, gathering as many of the documents and photographs as she could fit into her bag.

"Let's move," she said, slinging the bag over her shoulder. "We'll decode the rest of this later. But right now, we need to keep going."

Marcus led the way back toward the tunnel, his flashlight cutting through the darkness. As they left the antechamber behind, Eliza couldn't shake the feeling that they were moving closer to the heart of the Order's plans—and to a truth more dangerous than she had imagined.

The tunnel seemed to stretch endlessly, its dark, uneven walls swallowing the faint light of their flashlights. The air grew heavier with every step, carrying an oppressive sense of foreboding that settled deep in Marcus's chest. He could hear Eliza's steady footsteps ahead of him, her resolve evident in the determined pace she kept. But the weight of their discoveries—and the dangers they had already encountered—was starting to wear on him.

"Eliza," he said, breaking the silence, his voice low and edged with concern. "We need to talk."

"About what?" she asked, not breaking her stride. Her tone was neutral, but there was a sharp edge to it, as if she already knew what was coming.

Marcus quickened his pace until he was walking beside her. "About this whole thing. The deeper we go, the more it feels like we're in over our heads."

Eliza shot him a sideways glance, her brow furrowed. "We've been in over our heads since the councilman's office, Marcus. What's your point?"

"My point," he said, stopping abruptly and grabbing her arm gently to halt her as well, "is that we're outnumbered, outgunned, and out of options. You're brilliant, Eliza, but you're not bulletproof. Neither am I. If we keep pushing forward without backup—"

"There is no backup!" she snapped, pulling her arm free. Her flashlight beam wavered as she gestured toward the tunnel ahead. "Who are we supposed to call, Marcus? The police? The government? You think they'll believe us? Or that they're not already compromised?"

Marcus sighed, dragging a hand through his hair. "I'm not saying we go to them. But there's got to be someone we can trust. Someone who can help us."

"And risk tipping off the Order in the process?" Eliza countered, her voice sharp. "We've made it this far because we've kept this between us. Bringing in someone else just increases the chance of us getting caught—or worse."

"And what happens if we don't bring anyone else in?" Marcus asked, his tone rising. "What happens when we walk into the next trap and don't make it out?"

Eliza's jaw tightened, her flashlight beam steadying as she turned away from him. "I can't think like that. If I stop to consider every possible way this could go wrong, I'll never move forward. And if I don't move forward, my mother's work, the truth—it all dies with me."

Marcus exhaled sharply, stepping in front of her again. "I get it, okay? I know this is personal for you. But if you're so focused on finishing what your mother started that you get yourself killed, then what's the point? The Order wins, and all of this is for nothing."

Her shoulders tensed, but she didn't respond immediately. When she finally spoke, her voice was quieter but no less firm. "I'm not going to die, Marcus. And I'm not going to let them win."

"You don't know that," he said, his tone softening slightly. "None of us do. That's the problem."

They stood in tense silence for a moment, the distant drip of water the only sound echoing through the tunnel. Eliza's gaze dropped to the ground, her flashlight beam illuminating the uneven stone beneath their feet.

"I need to do this," she said finally, her voice barely above a whisper. "If I don't, no one else will."

Marcus sighed, his frustration giving way to reluctant understanding. "And I'm not saying stop. I'm saying be smart about it. You're not alone in this, Eliza. You've got me, and I'm not going anywhere. But if we're going to face whatever's waiting in that central chamber, we need to go in with a plan—and a way out."

Eliza looked up at him, her eyes fierce but tinged with a hint of vulnerability. "You're right," she admitted reluctantly. "We do need a plan. But we can't stop now. Not when we're this close."

Marcus nodded, his expression softening. "Then let's keep moving. But promise me one thing."

"What?" she asked, her tone cautious.

"That you'll trust me to pull us out if things go south," he said. "No heroics. No martyrdom. We both make it out of here alive, or neither of us does."

She hesitated, then nodded. "Deal."

With the tension between them easing slightly, they resumed their journey, the tunnel narrowing again as it curved sharply to the right. Despite their agreement, Marcus couldn't shake the uneasy feeling settling in his gut. He trusted Eliza's brilliance and determination, but the danger they faced felt insurmountable.

As they pressed on, the glow of faintly etched symbols began to appear on the walls again, their eerie light casting distorted shadows. Eliza's resolve hardened at the sight, while Marcus silently vowed to keep his promise—to stand by her side, no matter how dark the path ahead became.

The tunnel widened into a small alcove, its rough stone walls lined with ancient-looking shelves. Dust-covered relics sat undisturbed, their faint outlines barely visible under Eliza's flashlight. The air here was colder, heavier, as though the space itself carried the weight of the secrets it held.

Eliza's footsteps slowed as her eyes scanned the shelves. "This is different," she murmured, stepping closer to the artifacts.

Marcus followed, his flashlight sweeping the room. "Different how? It looks like more of the same—old junk the Order forgot to clean up."

"No," Eliza said, her voice sharpening. "This is personal."

She reached for a small, tarnished box nestled between two stacks of brittle papers. Its surface was etched with symbols that matched those in her mother's journal. Her pulse quickened as she carefully opened the box, her hands trembling slightly.

Inside was a simple locket, its once-polished surface dulled with age. Eliza froze, her breath catching in her throat as recognition dawned.

"Is that—?" Marcus began, stepping closer.

"It's hers," Eliza said softly, lifting the locket from the box. She turned it over in her hands, her flashlight revealing the faint initials engraved on the back: *M.K.*

Her mother's initials.

"Eliza," Marcus said cautiously, his voice cutting through the silence. "How can you be sure? It could've belonged to anyone."

She shook her head, her grip tightening on the locket. "I'm sure. She wore this every day. It was a gift from my father." Her voice wavered, but her resolve hardened as she slipped the locket into her pocket. "She was here, Marcus. Before she died, she was here."

Marcus frowned, glancing at the other artifacts scattered around the room. "If that's true, it means she got deeper into this than we thought. And if the Order knew she was here…"

"They killed her for it," Eliza finished, her voice cold. "They didn't just silence her—they wanted to erase her."

"Eliza, listen to me," Marcus said, stepping into her line of sight. "This doesn't change the fact that we're walking straight into their territory. If your mother was here and didn't make it out…"

"I'm not her," Eliza interrupted, meeting his gaze. "I have her notes, her warnings. I know more than she did when she was here."

"That doesn't make you invincible," Marcus said, his tone sharp. "The Order isn't playing games. They've been protecting this for decades—maybe longer. If we keep going, we're crossing a line we can't come back from."

"Good," Eliza said firmly. "Because that's exactly what I intend to do."

Marcus sighed, his frustration evident, but he didn't argue further. "All right," he said finally. "But let's be clear: if things go south, we pull back. No heroics, no stubborn last stands."

"Agreed," Eliza said, though the fire in her eyes suggested otherwise.

They resumed their search, the locket burning like a brand in Eliza's pocket. Her mother's presence in this place—her connection to the Order's secrets—was no longer just a theory. It was fact. And it gave her the resolve she needed to keep moving forward, no matter the danger.

Marcus's flashlight paused on a set of documents stacked haphazardly on a nearby shelf. He flipped through them quickly, his expression darkening. "These look like schematics," he said, holding them out to Eliza. "For some kind of machinery. Big machinery."

Eliza scanned the papers, her eyes narrowing. "Synchronization apparatus," she muttered, recognizing the terminology from her mother's journal. "This ties directly to the experiments. Whatever they're doing in the central chamber, it's massive."

"And it's probably the reason they didn't want your mother getting too close," Marcus said.

"Which means we're close," Eliza replied, her voice steely. She folded the schematics and tucked them into her bag, her gaze locked on the tunnel ahead. "Closer than anyone's been in years."

Marcus rested a hand on her shoulder, forcing her to pause. "Just promise me one thing," he said, his tone quieter now.

"What?"

"Promise me you'll keep your head," he said. "This isn't just about finding answers anymore. It's about staying alive long enough to do something with them."

Eliza hesitated, then nodded. "I promise."

But as they moved deeper into the tunnel, the weight of the locket in her pocket reminded her of what was at stake. Her mother had been here, fighting the same fight, chasing the same truth. Now, it was Eliza's turn to finish what she had started. And she would—no matter what stood in her way.

Chapter 13
The Core of the Conspiracy

The air in the tunnel felt heavier as Eliza and Marcus neared the coordinates marked on the stolen map. The faint glow of symbols on the walls grew brighter, pulsing faintly as though alive. Every step forward felt like a step deeper into the heart of the unknown, each moment tinged with the electric charge of impending danger.

Marcus's flashlight cut through the darkness, the beam bouncing off the damp stone walls. His posture was tense, his hand resting lightly on the grip of his weapon. "We're close," he said, his voice barely above a whisper. "Too close."

Eliza nodded, her own flashlight scanning the path ahead. Her focus was sharp, her resolve hardened by the discovery of her mother's locket. "Stay sharp," she replied. "If the Order's protecting something, this is where we'll find it."

Suddenly, a faint scuff echoed from the shadows ahead. Marcus stopped in his tracks, his flashlight whipping toward the sound. "Did you hear that?"

Eliza froze, her heart pounding in her chest. "I heard it," she whispered, her eyes narrowing as she adjusted her grip on the flashlight.

Before they could react further, two figures emerged from the darkness. Their faces were obscured by black masks, their movements swift and deliberate. One of them raised a metal rod, the faint glint of a blade catching in the beam of Marcus's flashlight.

"Run—" Marcus started, but the word barely escaped his lips before the first figure lunged.

The clash of metal against stone rang through the tunnel as Marcus deflected the blow with his flashlight, the force sending sparks skittering across the floor. Eliza stumbled backward, her flashlight tumbling from her grip as the second masked figure advanced on her.

"Eliza!" Marcus shouted, his voice tight with exertion.

"I've got this!" she yelled back, her hand darting into her bag. She pulled out her multi-tool, flipping open the blade just in time to block a strike aimed at her side. The masked figure snarled, their movements quick and precise, forcing her to retreat.

Marcus swung his flashlight like a club, connecting with the first attacker's arm. The figure staggered, but only for a moment before pressing forward again, their strikes relentless. "These guys aren't messing around!" he grunted, narrowly avoiding a slash to his shoulder.

"Neither are we," Eliza shot back, ducking under a swipe from her own assailant. She lashed out with her blade, catching the edge of the figure's sleeve. The fabric tore, revealing a faint tattoo beneath—a symbol she recognized immediately. The Order.

Her distraction cost her. The masked figure capitalized on her hesitation, slamming into her with enough force to knock her into the wall. Stars danced in her vision as she hit the stone, her breath leaving her in a sharp gasp.

"Eliza!" Marcus roared, turning just in time to see her attacker raising their weapon for another strike. Without hesitation, he drew his gun and fired. The shot rang out, deafening in the confined space, and the masked figure crumpled to the ground.

The remaining assailant hesitated, their masked face turning toward Marcus. They raised their blade as if to charge, but Marcus leveled his weapon at them, his stance unyielding. "Try it," he growled.

The figure hesitated for a fraction of a second before retreating into the shadows. The sound of their footsteps faded quickly, leaving only the ringing of the gunshot echoing through the tunnel.

Eliza pushed herself to her feet, wincing as she clutched her side. "Nice timing," she said, her voice strained.

"You okay?" Marcus asked, his concern cutting through the tension in his tone.

"Bruised, not broken," she replied, brushing dust off her jacket. She glanced at the crumpled form of the masked attacker, her gaze hard. "Whoever they are, they're not amateurs."

"No kidding," Marcus said, holstering his weapon. He grimaced as he shifted his weight, his hand instinctively going to his side.

Eliza's eyes narrowed. "Marcus. You're hit."

"It's nothing," he said quickly, though the blood seeping through his shirt told a different story.

"Let me see," she said, stepping closer.

"We don't have time for this," Marcus argued, though he didn't stop her as she pulled his shirt aside to inspect the wound.

The gash was deep but not fatal, the blood sluggish but steady. "You need this wrapped," she said, pulling a bandage from her bag.

"Do it fast," Marcus said through gritted teeth. "We need to keep moving. If there's one thing we know about the Order, it's that they never work alone."

Eliza worked quickly, her hands steady despite the adrenaline still coursing through her veins. "This better hold," she said, tying off the bandage. "But you're not invincible, Marcus. Don't push it."

He gave her a faint smile, though his eyes were serious. "I could say the same to you."

She nodded, retrieving her flashlight and bag. The fight had rattled her, but it had also steeled her resolve. The Order was willing to kill to protect their secrets, but that only made her more determined to uncover the truth.

"Let's move," she said, her voice firm. "The central chamber is close. Whatever they're hiding, we're going to find it."

Marcus nodded, his steps slower but no less determined as they continued down the tunnel. The encounter had left them shaken but unbroken, their resolve stronger than ever as they pushed deeper into the heart of the conspiracy.

The central chamber was larger than Eliza had imagined. Its high, arched ceiling was carved directly into the bedrock, with faintly glowing symbols etched into the walls. The room was lit by scattered, flickering work lights attached to modern machinery—an unsettling blend of ancient mysticism and cutting-edge technology.

Eliza's flashlight swept across the space, landing on a row of chemical vats lined neatly against one wall. Beside them, a series of workstations held technical schematics, documents, and what appeared to be samples of the same residue she had found on the councilman's hand.

"This is it," Eliza murmured, stepping further into the chamber. "This is where it all comes together."

Marcus followed, his hand still resting near the bandaged wound on his side. "It's bigger than I thought," he said, his voice low. "They've been running an operation down here for years, maybe decades."

Eliza approached one of the workstations, her gaze locking onto a set of schematics spread out across the table. She scanned the diagrams with her glasses, her mind racing to piece together their purpose. "These designs," she said, pointing to the intricate drawings. "They're for synchronization devices. The same ones my mother mentioned in her notes."

Marcus frowned, leaning over her shoulder. "Synchronization devices? For what?"

"To amplify something," she replied, her tone tight. "Energy, maybe. Or signals. Whatever it is, it's tied to the experiments."

"And the councilman?" Marcus asked, glancing at a stack of documents nearby.

Eliza picked up the topmost document, her eyes narrowing as she read. "He knew," she said, her voice sharpening. "He found out about the experiments. About what they were doing down here."

Marcus raised an eyebrow. "What exactly were they doing?"

"Testing," Eliza replied, her gaze locked on the page. "On people. It says here they were trying to find... compatibility with their 'legacy energy.'" She paused, her stomach twisting as she read further. "The residue. It's part of the process. They were exposing subjects to it to... synchronize them."

Marcus shook his head, disbelief evident in his voice. "Synchronize them? For what purpose?"

"To control them," Eliza said grimly. "To make them part of the convergence."

Marcus ran a hand down his face, exhaling sharply. "And the councilman found out about this?"

She nodded, picking up another document. It was a letter addressed to a high-ranking Order member, dated only weeks before the councilman's death. "'Councilman Renner has become a liability,'" she read aloud, her voice hardening. "'He is actively working to dismantle our operations, and his position grants him access to resources we cannot allow him to use against us. The matter must be resolved immediately.'"

Marcus's jaw tightened. "They killed him because he was trying to stop them."

"And because he was getting too close to the truth," Eliza added. She set the letter down, her fists clenching. "They didn't just silence him—they erased him. They made sure no one would ask questions."

Marcus scanned the room, his eyes narrowing. "So, what's the plan here? What's the convergence? And why go to all this trouble?"

Eliza hesitated, her gaze drifting to a set of monitors displaying data from the chemical vats. "The convergence isn't just about secrecy," she said finally. "It's about control. Synchronization, energy manipulation—it's all designed to centralize power. To make the Order untouchable."

"And everyone else?" Marcus asked, his tone dark.

"Expendable," Eliza replied, her voice cold. "The councilman wasn't just a threat—he was proof that their system could be disrupted. They couldn't afford to let him succeed."

Marcus sighed, running a hand through his hair. "So, what now? We've got evidence, but no way to stop this on our own."

"We don't need to stop it all at once," Eliza said, her gaze fierce. "We just need to expose them. To make sure the world knows what they're doing."

Marcus raised an eyebrow. "And how exactly are we going to do that?"

"By taking this," Eliza replied, gesturing to the documents and schematics. "Everything they've worked to hide is right here. We collect it, we get out, and we find a way to broadcast the truth."

"And if they find us first?" Marcus asked, his tone edged with skepticism.

"Then we don't let them," Eliza said firmly. "We've come too far to back down now."

Marcus studied her for a moment, then nodded. "All right. But we do this smart. No more close calls."

Eliza allowed herself a faint smile. "Agreed."

As they began gathering the evidence, the gravity of their discovery settled over them. The councilman's death, her mother's warnings, the Order's experiments—it all pointed to a single truth: the convergence was imminent, and the Order would stop at nothing to see it succeed.

But for the first time, Eliza felt the odds tipping in their favor. They had the proof. Now, they just needed to survive long enough to use it.

The sudden hum of machinery filled the chamber, breaking the silence. Eliza and Marcus froze, their eyes darting toward the source of the sound. A projector mounted on the far wall whirred to life, its light casting a sharp, flickering glow against the rough stone surface.

"What now?" Marcus muttered, instinctively stepping closer to Eliza.

The projector flickered, and an image sharpened into view—a masked figure seated at a high-backed chair, their posture commanding and deliberate. Behind them, faintly glowing symbols lined the wall, their patterns eerily familiar to Eliza. Her stomach tightened as recognition set in.

"Welcome," the figure said, their voice distorted but clear, reverberating through the chamber. "To those foolish enough to trespass into the heart of the Concordant Order, consider this your first and only warning."

Eliza's fingers tightened around the edge of the table, her mind racing. The voice was calm, measured, but laced with an undercurrent of menace.

"Leave now," the figure continued, "or face the full weight of the consequences. The convergence is inevitable. You cannot stop it. You cannot understand it. And you will not survive if you attempt to interfere further."

Marcus scoffed, his arms crossing over his chest. "Real welcoming bunch, aren't they?"

"Quiet," Eliza said sharply, her gaze locked on the screen. Her attention drifted to the symbols etched into the wall behind the masked figure. They weren't just decorations—they were identical to the sketches in her mother's journal, the same ones she had seen in the tunnels and scattered throughout the Order's documents.

"Do you see that?" she whispered, pointing to the symbols.

Marcus frowned, leaning closer. "Yeah. Looks like their usual cryptic nonsense."

"No," Eliza said, her voice tight. "It's more than that. These are the same symbols my mother documented. The same ones she warned about."

Marcus's expression darkened. "You're saying she knew about all this? The leader? The convergence?"

"Maybe not everything," Eliza admitted, her voice tinged with frustration. "But she was close—closer than anyone else has been."

The figure on the screen leaned forward slightly, as if addressing them directly. "You have seen enough to know that your interference will only bring ruin. Leave now, and we may yet allow you to disappear unnoticed. Stay, and you will suffer the same fate as those before you."

"Subtle," Marcus muttered, though his grip on his weapon tightened.

Eliza's mind raced, piecing together the threads of what she was seeing. The symbols, the message, the threats—it all pointed to one thing: the Order's leader was not only aware of their presence but also deeply tied to the history her mother had uncovered.

"They're trying to scare us off," she said finally, her voice steady.

"Yeah, well, it's working," Marcus replied, glancing toward the tunnel they had entered through. "What's the plan, Kain? Because I'm not liking our odds if this goes south."

"We don't leave," Eliza said firmly. "Not yet. There's more here—something my mother was trying to find. Something they're still trying to hide."

The projector's image flickered, the figure's masked face momentarily distorting. "You have been warned," the voice said, their tone unyielding. "Your lives are inconsequential. The convergence cannot be stopped."

As the message faded, the projector whirred to a stop, plunging the chamber into silence once more.

Marcus exhaled sharply, his flashlight sweeping the room. "Well, that was cheery. Any chance they'll back up their threats with an actual welcome party?"

"Count on it," Eliza said, her tone grim. She moved quickly to the table, her fingers brushing over the documents and schematics they had been examining earlier. "But we're not leaving without this. This evidence is the only thing that can expose them."

Marcus shook his head, frustration flashing across his face. "Eliza, you just heard them. They know we're here. They're probably already on their way."

"Good," she said, slipping the documents into her bag. "Let them come. The more desperate they get, the more mistakes they'll make."

He sighed, but there was no mistaking the resolve in his expression. "Fine. But if this gets us killed, I'm haunting you."

Eliza smirked faintly, though the tension in her posture remained. "Deal. Now help me grab the rest of this."

As they worked quickly to collect the remaining evidence, Eliza couldn't shake the image of the symbols from her mind. Her mother's connection to the Order was no longer just a possibility—it was a certainty. And with every step closer to the truth, the stakes grew higher.

The convergence was imminent. The Order was watching. But Eliza refused to back down. Whatever secrets lay ahead, she was determined to uncover them—no matter the cost.

The faint tremor beneath Eliza's feet was the first warning. She froze mid-step, her flashlight beam wavering as small bits of dust and debris rained from the ceiling of the central chamber.

"Did you feel that?" she asked, her voice tight.

Marcus, crouched by a workstation with a handful of documents, looked up sharply. "Feel it? I think I just saw it." He gestured toward the faintly swaying machinery along the walls. "That's not normal."

Eliza stepped toward him, scanning the room with her forensic glasses. Her heart sank as she picked up faint traces of explosive residue embedded in the walls. "They've rigged it," she said, her voice laced with urgency.

"Rigged it?" Marcus echoed, rising to his feet.

"This whole chamber—it's set to blow," she said, grabbing the nearest stack of papers and shoving them into her bag. "They're not just protecting their secrets; they're erasing them."

Another tremor shook the room, this one stronger than the last. A loud creak echoed through the space, followed by a deep, ominous rumble. Marcus swore under his breath, his flashlight beam darting toward the ceiling as more debris fell.

"We need to move, now," he said, his voice sharp.

Eliza hesitated, her gaze darting between the remaining evidence and the exit. "I'm not leaving without—"

"Eliza!" Marcus snapped, grabbing her arm. "If we don't get out of here, there won't be anything left of us to take evidence back."

She bit her lip, the weight of his words crashing against her determination. The floor beneath them groaned, a jagged crack splitting through the stone and sending chunks of rock tumbling into the abyss below.

"Fine," she said reluctantly. "Let's go."

They ran toward the tunnel they had entered through, their footsteps echoing in the collapsing chamber. The air grew thick with dust, making it harder to see and even harder to breathe.

Marcus glanced over his shoulder, his voice strained. "You think they triggered this remotely?"

"Does it matter?" Eliza shot back, clutching her bag tightly. "They're not giving us time to figure it out."

A deafening boom shook the ground, throwing them off balance. Marcus stumbled, catching himself against the wall. "That sounded close," he said, his voice laced with alarm.

"It was," Eliza replied grimly, helping him steady himself. "Keep moving."

As they neared the exit, a massive piece of the ceiling collapsed behind them, sending a cloud of debris surging forward. The force of the impact knocked them both to the ground.

"Eliza!" Marcus called, coughing as he scrambled to his feet. "Are you okay?"

"I'm fine," she said, her voice muffled by the dust. She pushed herself up, her bag still clutched in her hand. "But we're out of time."

They sprinted the last few meters to the tunnel, the chamber behind them collapsing in on itself. The roaring sound of destruction filled the air, drowning out even their labored breaths.

The moment they crossed into the tunnel, Marcus grabbed Eliza's arm and pulled her forward. "Come on! This whole place could go!"

They didn't stop until they were far enough from the collapsing chamber that the rumbling had become a distant echo. Both of them leaned against the tunnel walls, gasping for breath, their faces streaked with dust and sweat.

"That," Marcus said between breaths, "was too close."

Eliza nodded, her hands trembling as she opened her bag. She pulled out a stack of documents, the edges singed and covered in dust. "We didn't get everything," she said, her voice heavy with frustration.

"No," Marcus agreed, glancing at the papers. "But you got enough. It's something."

"It's not enough to stop them," Eliza said, shaking her head. "They destroyed the chamber, the evidence, everything that could prove what they're planning."

Marcus rested a hand on her shoulder, his voice steady despite the tension in his posture. "We'll figure it out. You've still got pieces. We'll put them together."

Eliza looked at him, her expression softening. "We don't have much time. The convergence is happening soon—I can feel it."

"Then we move fast," Marcus said. "But first, we get out of here alive. Agreed?"

She nodded reluctantly, slipping the documents back into her bag. "Agreed."

As they made their way through the tunnels, the weight of their near-death experience settled heavily over them. The Order had made it clear—they were willing to destroy anything, and anyone, to protect their secrets.

But as shaken as Eliza felt, her resolve only grew stronger. They had survived. And with the fragments they had salvaged, she would find a way to stop the Order before it was too late.

Chapter 14
Unveiling the Experiment

The hum of Eliza's forensic scanner filled the lab as she hovered it over the charred edges of the salvaged documents. Her workspace was cluttered with maps, schematics, and notes scrawled in hurried handwriting, each piece a fragment of the puzzle she was desperate to solve. The faint glow of her computer screens cast sharp shadows across her face, reflecting her intense focus.

"Anything?" Marcus asked, his voice breaking the tense silence. He leaned against the edge of the desk, his arm still wrapped tightly from the injury he'd sustained in the tunnels.

"Give me a minute," Eliza replied, her eyes darting over the scanned text. "These documents are coded, but they're using the same patterns as my mother's notes. If I can match the symbols..." She trailed off, her fingers flying over the keyboard.

Marcus exhaled, running a hand through his hair. "Look, I know you're in your element, but we don't exactly have the luxury of time here. If the Order knows we survived, they'll be coming for us."

"I'm aware," Eliza snapped, her frustration bleeding into her tone. She sighed, shaking her head. "Sorry. It's just—this isn't just about stopping them. It's about understanding what they're planning."

"And you think these papers will tell you that?" Marcus asked, gesturing to the scattered documents.

"They have to," she said, her voice firm. "Look at this." She pointed to a section of text that her scanner had translated. "'Synchronization points identified. Energy fields stabilized. Preparations underway for final convergence.'"

Marcus frowned, his brow furrowing. "Synchronization points? Energy fields? What does that even mean?"

"It means they're coordinating something massive," Eliza replied. She grabbed a map from the desk, its surface marked with red circles around key locations in the city. "These are the synchronization points. The tunnels, the councilman's office, the abandoned factory—they're all part of the same network."

Marcus leaned closer, his gaze narrowing. "And this 'convergence'—what is it? Some kind of mass experiment?"

"That's exactly what it is," Eliza said, her voice grim. "These documents reference a large-scale event designed to influence the city's population. Energy manipulation, chemical dispersal—it's all here."

Marcus's jaw tightened. "Influence them how?"

"To control them," she said simply, her eyes meeting his. "To turn them into... extensions of the Order's will."

He stared at her, disbelief flashing across his face. "That's insane."

"It's brilliant," Eliza corrected, though her voice was laced with disgust. "The Order isn't just protecting their secrets—they're creating a system that ensures no one can challenge them. A synchronized population, completely subservient to their plans."

Marcus shook his head, stepping away from the desk. "And the councilman was trying to stop this?"

"Yes," Eliza said, pulling another document from the pile. "He found out about the experiments and tried to dismantle their network. But they silenced him before he could expose them."

"And your mother?" Marcus asked, his voice quieter now.

"She must have found out, too," Eliza replied, her fingers tracing the edge of the map. "Her notes weren't just research—they were warnings. She knew this was coming."

Marcus paced the length of the room, his movements restless. "So, what do we do now? We've got evidence, but it's not like we can walk into a newsroom and spill everything."

Eliza's eyes lit up with determination. "We don't need to expose everything—not yet. We just need to disrupt the convergence. If we can stop the event, we buy ourselves time to gather more evidence and bring the Order down for good."

"And how exactly do we stop it?" Marcus asked, his tone skeptical. "You just said it's a massive operation spread across the entire city."

Eliza gestured to the map. "The central chamber was their hub. Without it, they'll be scrambling to coordinate. If we can identify the key points—locations where the synchronization devices are active—we can disable them."

Marcus stopped pacing, crossing his arms as he studied her. "You really think this will work?"

"It has to," she said, her voice unwavering. "If we don't stop this, they win. The city becomes their experiment, and no one will even know it happened."

He sighed, nodding reluctantly. "All right. But if we're doing this, we do it together. No solo missions, no reckless stunts."

Eliza smirked faintly, though her focus remained on the map. "Deal."

As Marcus stepped back to give her room to work, Eliza's mind raced. The pieces were finally coming together, but the stakes had never been higher. The Order's plans were larger than she had ever imagined, and the clock was ticking. But for the first time, she felt a glimmer of hope. They had the knowledge. Now, they just needed the courage to act.

Marcus winced as he adjusted his bandaged arm, leaning heavily against the edge of Eliza's cluttered desk. His exhaustion was evident, but the intensity in his gaze was sharper than ever. Eliza barely looked up from her monitor, her fingers flying across the keyboard as she decrypted another set of files. The tension in the room was palpable.

"Eliza," Marcus said, his voice firm but low.

"Not now," she replied curtly, her eyes fixed on the screen.

"Yes, now," Marcus insisted, pushing off the desk and stepping closer. "We need to talk."

Eliza exhaled sharply, finally turning to face him. "What is it, Marcus? Because unless it's about stopping the convergence, it can wait."

"It's about survival," Marcus said, his tone hardening. "We're not just fighting some secret club of conspirators anymore. The Order knows who we are. They know where we've been, and after that stunt in the tunnels, you can bet they're coming for us."

She straightened, crossing her arms. "You think I don't know that? We're visible targets, sure. But running to the authorities won't fix that."

Marcus took a step closer, his frustration evident. "We've got enough evidence now. Documents, schematics, even that creepy message from their leader. If we go to the authorities—someone outside their reach—we might actually stand a chance at taking them down."

Eliza shook her head, her expression resolute. "And who exactly do you think is outside their reach? The Order's been operating for decades, Marcus. You think they don't have people in law enforcement? In government?"

"That's a hell of an assumption," he shot back. "Not everyone's on their payroll."

"Maybe not," she admitted, her voice softening slightly. "But how do we know who to trust? What if we go to the wrong person and end up handing everything over to the Order?"

Marcus opened his mouth to argue but stopped, running a hand through his hair instead. "I get it," he said finally. "I do. But we can't keep doing this alone. You saw how close we came in that chamber. We can't afford another close call."

Eliza sighed, her gaze dropping to the desk. She absently ran her fingers over the edges of a schematic, her thoughts racing. "I'm not saying we do this alone forever," she said quietly. "But we need to be smart about who we bring into this. One wrong move, and it's over."

"And what happens if we wait too long?" Marcus asked, his voice softening but still firm. "This convergence thing—it's not some far-off theory. It's happening, and soon. If we don't act fast, it won't matter who we trust or don't trust."

She looked up at him, her jaw tightening. "I know that, Marcus. But I need time to figure out our next move. To make sure we're not walking into another trap."

"We don't have time," Marcus said, shaking his head. "Look, I'll admit you're smarter than me when it comes to all this—"

He gestured vaguely at the documents and screens. "—but even you can't outthink them forever. At some point, you have to take a leap and trust someone."

Eliza met his gaze, her expression unreadable. "And what if that someone betrays us? What if they're already part of the Order?"

"Then we deal with it," Marcus replied, his tone calm but resolute. "But sitting here, waiting for them to find us? That's not a plan, Eliza. That's suicide."

The room fell into a tense silence, broken only by the faint hum of the computer. Eliza turned back to the monitor, her fingers hovering over the keyboard. "I'm not ready to make that call," she said finally. "Not yet."

Marcus let out a slow breath, his frustration giving way to reluctant understanding. "Fine," he said, stepping back. "But if we're not going to the authorities, we need a contingency plan. Somewhere to go if they find us here."

"I'll figure it out," she replied, her focus already shifting back to the files.

"Not later," Marcus said firmly. "Now."

Eliza glanced at him, her lips pressing into a thin line. She nodded once, reluctantly. "All right. I'll start working on it."

"Good," Marcus said, leaning heavily against the wall. "Because I don't plan on dying in this lab, Kain. And neither should you."

His words hung in the air as Eliza returned to her work, her mind torn between deciphering the Order's plans and the weight of Marcus's warning. The stakes had never been higher, and the margin for error had never been smaller.

But one thing was clear: they couldn't afford to fail.

The steady rhythm of Eliza's typing came to an abrupt halt as a notification blinked on her screen. She leaned closer, her brow furrowing at the unexpected sight of an encrypted message. It had bypassed her firewall, an almost impossible feat considering the layers of security she had built.

"What is it?" Marcus asked, noticing her tense posture.

Eliza hesitated, her fingers hovering over the keyboard. "I don't know. It's an encrypted message—anonymous sender. Whoever it is, they know their way around high-level security."

Marcus stepped closer, his arms crossing as he studied the screen. "And we're just going to open it? Sounds like a trap."

"Or a lead," Eliza countered. "Give me a second."

Her fingers moved swiftly, decrypting the message with a series of commands. The text unfolded line by line, revealing a concise and chilling message:

I know what you've found. I know what you're trying to stop. I was part of the Order once. If you want to expose them, I can help. But be warned: what you're walking into is far more dangerous than you realize.

Eliza read the words aloud, her voice steady despite the knot tightening in her chest.

Marcus shook his head immediately. "No way. We don't trust this. Whoever sent that could be trying to lure us into another trap."

"Maybe," Eliza said, her eyes narrowing as she reread the message. "But whoever it is, they know about the Order. They know enough to reach me, to bypass my security. That's not random."

"Exactly," Marcus replied, his voice rising slightly. "They're too good. Doesn't that scream 'set-up' to you?"

Eliza tilted her head, her mind racing. "Or it means they're legitimate. Someone on the inside could be trying to help us."

Marcus scoffed, pacing behind her. "The same way the Order helped your mother? Or the councilman? Come on, Eliza. We're talking about a group that silences anyone who gets too close. Why would they suddenly have a whistleblower?"

"Because cracks form in every system," Eliza shot back, turning in her chair to face him. "Maybe this person saw what the Order was doing and decided they couldn't be part of it anymore. It happens."

"Or maybe they're baiting us," Marcus said firmly. "Waiting for us to trust them so they can finish what they started in that chamber."

Eliza sighed, pinching the bridge of her nose. "I get it, Marcus. I do. But we can't afford to ignore this. If this person really was part of the Order, they could have information we'll never find on our own."

"And if they're lying?" Marcus asked, his tone sharp. "If this is just another way to get to us?"

"Then we'll handle it," she said, her voice hardening. "But we can't stop moving forward because we're afraid of what might happen. The convergence is happening, and we're running out of time."

He studied her for a long moment, the tension between them thick. Finally, he let out a resigned sigh. "Fine. But if we're doing this, we do it carefully. No face-to-face meetings, no sharing everything we've got."

"Agreed," Eliza said quickly, turning back to the screen. She began typing a response, her fingers steady despite the weight of the decision.

Who are you? And why should we trust you?

The reply came almost immediately, a single line of text that sent a chill down Eliza's spine.

I worked with your mother. I know how she died.

Eliza's hands froze over the keyboard, her breath catching in her throat. She stared at the words, her mind swirling with questions and emotions she couldn't yet name.

Marcus leaned over her shoulder, his expression dark. "Eliza, this feels wrong."

"I have to know," she said quietly. "If they knew my mother—if they can tell me what happened to her…"

"That's exactly what they're counting on," Marcus warned. "Don't let them manipulate you."

She nodded, though her resolve didn't waver. She typed another response, her tone measured but firm:

Prove it. Tell me something only someone close to her would know.

There was a pause, longer this time, and Eliza held her breath as the screen refreshed.

The locket she wore. Inside was a photo of you as a child. She said it kept her strong.

Eliza's heart tightened. It was true—her mother's locket, the one she had found in the tunnels, held the very picture the sender described.

Marcus swore under his breath, stepping back. "That doesn't prove anything. It's common knowledge she had a kid."

"It's more than that," Eliza murmured, her voice barely above a whisper. "This person knew about the locket, about what it meant to her. That's not something the Order would care to fabricate."

Marcus sighed, running a hand through his hair. "All right. Let's say they're telling the truth. What's their endgame?"

Eliza's jaw tightened as she typed her final message. *If you're serious about helping, send more details. We'll decide what to do from there.*

The screen remained silent for a moment before the reply came through:

Check the tunnel map. There's a hidden chamber beneath the East Sector. That's where you'll find the proof you need.

Eliza leaned back, her mind racing. The East Sector wasn't marked on any of the maps she had decoded so far, but it aligned with some of the gaps in the Order's network.

"We have a lead," she said, her voice filled with quiet determination.

"And a trap," Marcus added grimly.

"Maybe," Eliza admitted. "But it's the best chance we've got."

Marcus exhaled slowly, his gaze steady. "Then let's make sure we're ready for whatever's waiting down there."

Eliza nodded, her resolve hardening. The stakes had never been higher, but with this new ally—or enemy—on the horizon, she felt closer to the truth than ever.

The glow of the computer screen cast sharp shadows across the lab as Eliza hunched over the map spread out on the desk. Red circles and lines crisscrossed the layout, each one representing a potential point of entry, a synchronization site, or a hazard. Her pen moved quickly, jotting notes in the margins while her mind worked at a frantic pace.

Behind her, Marcus leaned against the counter, watching her with a mixture of admiration and unease. His arm was still bandaged, but he looked more alert now, the grim determination in his eyes matching her own.

"Eliza," he said finally, breaking the silence. "You've been at this for hours. When's the last time you stopped to breathe?"

She didn't look up, her voice clipped. "Breathing isn't going to stop the convergence, Marcus."

"No, but running yourself into the ground might," he countered, stepping closer. "You can't do this alone, no matter how many maps you draw or plans you make."

"I'm not doing it alone," she replied sharply, her gaze flicking up to meet his. "You're here, aren't you?"

"For now," Marcus said, gesturing to the chaotic mess of papers and equipment around them. "But this? This is starting to look less like a plan and more like a suicide mission."

Eliza straightened, her hands braced on the edge of the desk. "It's only a suicide mission if we fail. And I don't plan on failing."

Marcus let out a sharp breath, crossing his arms. "Okay, but let's be real for a second. We're talking about infiltrating one of the most secretive, dangerous organizations in existence. They've already tried to kill us more than once. What makes you think this time will be any different?"

She stepped around the desk, grabbing a small toolkit and stuffing it into her bag. "Because this time, we're ready. We know where they're vulnerable, and we know what they're planning. They don't expect us to fight back."

"Maybe not," Marcus said, following her. "But they'll be ready for anything. And we're two people, Eliza. Two."

"Two is enough," she said firmly, checking the straps on her bag. "I've done more with less."

"That was before the stakes were this high," Marcus argued, his voice rising. "Before you had someone to watch your back."

Eliza paused, her expression softening for a brief moment. "I know the risks, Marcus. But if we don't act now, we lose everything. The city, the truth—it's all gone. They'll win."

"And what happens if we don't make it out?" he asked, his tone quieter now. "What happens then?"

She turned back to the desk, picking up the locket she had found in the tunnels. Her fingers brushed over the worn surface as she spoke. "Then we make sure someone else can finish what we started."

Marcus stared at her, his jaw tightening. "That's not exactly comforting."

"It's not supposed to be," she said, tucking the locket into her pocket. "This isn't about comfort. It's about stopping them, no matter what it takes."

The silence between them was heavy, broken only by the faint hum of the lab's equipment. Marcus finally stepped forward, his voice low but steady. "You're sure about this?"

She met his gaze, her eyes burning with determination. "This isn't just about me anymore," she said. "It's about everyone they've hurt, everyone they've controlled. It's about making sure they don't get to do it again."

Marcus nodded slowly, his expression grim but resolute. "Then let's make it count."

Eliza gave him a faint smile, her focus already shifting back to the map. She picked up the pen and circled one final point—the East Sector, the location mentioned in the anonymous message.

"This is where it starts," she said, her voice firm. "And this is where it ends."

As the two of them prepared to leave, the weight of what lay ahead pressed heavily on their shoulders. The risks were immense, the odds stacked against them. But for the first time, Eliza felt the faintest glimmer of hope. They were no longer running—they were fighting back. And she was ready.

Chapter 15
The Final Move

The tunnel narrowed as Eliza and Marcus approached the entrance to the Order's operational base. The faint hum of machinery and distant murmurs of voices grew louder with every step. Eliza adjusted her glasses, their enhanced mode scanning for hidden traps or surveillance devices. Beside her, Marcus checked his weapon, his movements tense but controlled.

"This is it," Eliza whispered, her voice barely audible over the faint echo of dripping water. "The base is just ahead."

Marcus leaned closer, his flashlight dimmed to a faint glow. "Are we sure about this tip? What if it's a setup?"

Eliza glanced at him, her jaw tight. "It's a risk we have to take. We've come too far to turn back now."

He exhaled sharply, nodding. "All right. Let's make it count."

They crept forward, the entrance to the base coming into view. A heavy steel door was embedded in the stone wall, its surface scratched and dented from years of use. Above it, a small surveillance camera pivoted slowly, scanning the corridor.

"Camera," Marcus muttered, nodding toward the device.

"I see it," Eliza said, pulling a small device from her bag. She crouched against the wall, her fingers working quickly to hack into the camera's feed. After a moment, the red light on the camera flickered and turned off. "It's disabled. Let's move."

Marcus pressed his ear to the door, listening for movement on the other side. "It's quiet," he whispered. "Too quiet."

Eliza scanned the door with her glasses, detecting faint traces of heat near the edges. "It's rigged," she said grimly. "Pressure sensors. If we force it, we trigger the alarm."

"Great," Marcus muttered. "Any ideas?"

Eliza smirked faintly, pulling out a set of tools. "Step back."

She worked quickly, bypassing the sensors with precision. The door released with a soft click, and she pushed it open just enough to peer inside. The corridor beyond was dimly lit, its walls lined with conduits and control panels.

"Clear," she said, slipping through the gap.

Marcus followed, his movements careful as he scanned their surroundings. "How big do you think this place is?" he asked.

"Big enough to run a citywide experiment," Eliza replied. "Stay focused."

They moved deeper into the facility, their footsteps silent on the concrete floor. The hum of machinery grew louder, interspersed with the occasional murmur of voices. Eliza's glasses picked up faint heat signatures ahead, marking the positions of two guards standing at an intersection.

"Two guards," she whispered, nodding toward the corner. "We'll have to take them out quietly."

Marcus nodded, gripping his weapon. "I'll take the left. You handle the right."

Eliza slipped ahead, her movements fluid and controlled. She crept up behind the guard on the right, disabling him with a quick strike to the back of the neck. Marcus did the same to the left, catching the unconscious man before he hit the floor.

"Nice work," Eliza said quietly, dragging the body out of sight.

"You too," Marcus replied, his breathing steady. "Let's keep moving."

As they navigated further into the facility, the environment became more sophisticated. The walls were lined with monitors displaying live feeds of various parts of the city, each one overlaid with data and coordinates. Eliza's stomach churned as she recognized some of the locations—synchronization points marked on her map.

"This is how they're monitoring the city," she said, her voice tight. "They've got everything mapped out."

Marcus frowned, scanning the screens. "What's this?" He pointed to a display showing a countdown. The timer had less than 24 hours remaining.

Eliza's heart sank. "It's the convergence. They're almost ready."

"Then we don't have time to waste," Marcus said. "Let's find what we need and get out of here."

Eliza nodded, pulling up a schematic of the facility on her glasses. "The main control room should be just ahead. If we can access their systems, we might be able to disrupt the convergence."

"And if we can't?" Marcus asked.

"Then we make sure this place doesn't survive the night," Eliza replied, her voice steely.

They pressed on, navigating past more traps and evading patrolling guards. Each step brought them closer to the heart of the Order's operation—and closer to the truth they had been chasing for so long.

But as they approached the control room, Eliza couldn't shake the feeling that they were walking into the lion's den. The stakes had never been higher, and every decision they made would determine not just their survival, but the fate of the entire city.

The central hub of the Order's headquarters was a sprawling room of cold metal and glowing screens. Banks of monitors displayed live feeds from across the city, each one marked with overlays of data—traffic patterns, energy flows, and synchronization points. The hum of machinery filled the air, and the faint scent of ozone lingered, adding to the sterile, oppressive atmosphere.

Eliza stepped cautiously into the room, her eyes scanning every detail. The plans she had pieced together were laid bare in front of her. Maps of the city adorned one wall, crisscrossed with red lines and symbols that mirrored those in her mother's journal.

"This is it," she murmured, her voice almost drowned out by the ambient noise. "This is the heart of their operation."

Marcus followed her inside, his hand resting on his weapon. "Feels like a bad sci-fi movie," he said, his voice low. "Except this is real. And it's worse."

Eliza approached one of the larger monitors, its screen filled with a countdown similar to the one they had seen earlier. The timer now showed less than twenty hours. She touched the edge of the console, her fingers trembling slightly as she accessed the system.

"They're not just monitoring the city," she said, her tone sharp. "They're controlling it. Look at this." She pointed to a map overlaid with pulsing signals. "These are synchronization nodes. They're positioned to influence energy fields across the entire city."

Marcus frowned, stepping closer. "Energy fields? What kind of influence are we talking about?"

"Psychological," Eliza replied, her voice tight. "They're using a combination of electromagnetic waves and chemical dispersal to manipulate emotions—fear, compliance, even loyalty. The convergence isn't just an experiment. It's a takeover."

Marcus exhaled sharply, running a hand through his hair. "They're turning the entire city into puppets."

"Exactly," Eliza said. She leaned over the console, scrolling through reams of data. "The councilman was trying to stop this. He found out about the synchronization process and tried to expose them. That's why they killed him."

"And your mother?" Marcus asked, his voice softer now.

Eliza froze, her heart pounding. "She knew," she whispered. "She was involved in this."

"What?" Marcus stepped beside her, his brow furrowing. "Eliza, what are you talking about?"

She opened another file, her breath catching as her mother's name appeared on the screen: *Dr. Margaret Kain—Lead Researcher, Synchronization Project.* Eliza's vision blurred as she read the words. "She was part of it," she said, her voice trembling. "She worked on the experiments."

Marcus hesitated, placing a hand on her shoulder. "Eliza, I'm sorry. But maybe she didn't have a choice. The Order doesn't seem like the type to take no for an answer."

"She had a choice," Eliza snapped, pulling away from him. Her fingers flew over the keyboard as she searched for more. "She knew what they were doing, Marcus. She knew, and she stayed."

"Maybe she stayed to stop it," Marcus said gently. "You said it yourself—she was trying to dismantle them."

Eliza paused, her gaze locking onto a personal log hidden deep within the system. She opened it, her mother's voice filling the room in a recorded message.

"If you're hearing this, it means I didn't make it. The synchronization project is more dangerous than even the Order realizes. They think they can control it, but they're wrong. The energy they're manipulating—it's unstable. It could destroy the city, maybe more. I've tried to sabotage the project, but they're watching me too closely. Eliza, if you ever find this... know that I'm sorry. I never wanted you to be part of this. But you're the only one who can stop it now. Be stronger than I was."

The recording ended, leaving a heavy silence in its wake.

Marcus spoke first, his voice barely above a whisper. "She tried, Eliza. She tried to stop them."

Eliza's hands clenched into fists, her mind racing. "She still worked for them," she said bitterly. "She still helped build this."

"And then she tried to tear it down," Marcus countered. "She risked her life to stop them. That has to mean something."

Eliza turned away from the monitor, her emotions swirling between anger and grief. "It doesn't change what they're doing," she said finally. "It doesn't change what we have to do."

"No," Marcus agreed, his tone steady. "But it explains why you're the one standing here now. She believed in you, Eliza. Enough to leave everything behind for you to find."

She nodded slowly, her resolve hardening. "Then we finish this," she said, her voice firm. "For her. For everyone they've hurt."

Marcus gave her a faint smile, his gaze unwavering. "Let's take them down."

Together, they began extracting the data, their movements precise and deliberate. The truth was undeniable now, and the stakes had never been higher. The convergence was looming, and the Order's control was almost absolute.

But Eliza was done running. It was time to fight back.

The air in the headquarters felt heavier, as if the walls themselves were closing in. Eliza and Marcus worked quickly, transferring the files from the Order's system to a portable drive. Each passing second made Eliza's pulse race faster, the weight of what they had uncovered pressing down on her shoulders.

"We're almost there," Eliza said, her voice tight with focus. The progress bar on the screen inched closer to completion, a lifeline in their desperate mission.

Marcus stood by the door, his weapon drawn and his eyes scanning the corridor beyond. "Let's hope we make it out before they notice," he said, his voice low but tense.

A soft chime from Eliza's glasses interrupted the fragile calm. A new message flashed across the heads-up display: *Your time is up.*

Her blood ran cold. "Marcus," she whispered, her voice barely audible.

He turned sharply, his grip tightening on his weapon. "What is it?"

Before she could answer, the sound of heavy footsteps echoed through the corridor. A voice crackled over the intercom, calm and cold. "You've done well to make it this far, Eliza. But the game ends here."

The voice was familiar—it belonged to their anonymous informant.

Marcus's jaw tightened as he looked at her. "Tell me this isn't happening."

Eliza's mind raced. "It was a trap," she said, her voice filled with bitter realization. "They baited us with the information. They wanted us here."

"Brilliant deduction," the voice mocked, its tone laced with smugness. "You've been a thorn in our side for too long. It's time to cut you out—for good."

A deafening alarm blared, and the corridor erupted with activity. Guards poured into the hallway, their weapons drawn, their movements precise. Marcus fired the first shot, taking down one of the attackers before grabbing Eliza's arm.

"Move!" he shouted, pulling her away from the console.

"But the files—" she began, her voice frantic.

"No time!" Marcus snapped, shoving her toward the side door. "We have what we need. Go!"

Eliza hesitated, her instincts screaming at her to stay and finish the download. But the look in Marcus's eyes left no room for argument. She sprinted toward the exit, the portable drive clutched tightly in her hand.

Behind her, Marcus stayed, his weapon blazing as he held off the advancing guards. "Go, Eliza!" he yelled, his voice echoing through the chaos. "I'll cover you!"

"Marcus!" she screamed, stopping at the door.

He turned toward her, his expression fierce. "Don't stop. Don't look back. You have to finish this."

Tears stung her eyes, but she nodded, her heart breaking as she obeyed. She slipped through the door, her mind racing as she navigated the labyrinthine corridors. The sound of gunfire and shouts grew fainter with every step, but the pain in her chest only deepened.

Eliza reached a maintenance hatch and climbed through, emerging into the cold night air. She collapsed against the wall, gasping for breath, the weight of the drive in her hand a cruel reminder of what Marcus had sacrificed.

For a moment, the world felt impossibly still. She clutched the drive tightly, her resolve hardening even as tears streamed down her face. "I'll finish this," she whispered, her voice trembling. "For him. For everyone."

The distant echo of an explosion snapped her back to reality. The Order's headquarters shook as flames erupted from within, consuming everything in its path.

Eliza's heart twisted, but she pushed herself to her feet. She couldn't stop now—not when so much had been lost. She had the evidence, the truth that could expose the Order once and for all. And she wouldn't let Marcus's sacrifice be in vain.

Wiping her tears, she disappeared into the shadows, her mind focused on the next step. The fight wasn't over—not yet. And she would make sure the Order paid for everything they had taken.

The pale light of dawn crept over the city as Eliza stepped out of the underground network. Her body ached with every movement, her clothes torn and bloodied. She leaned heavily against the nearest wall, the cool stone grounding her in the moment. Her mind raced with the weight of what she had lost—and what still lay ahead.

The portable drive in her hand felt impossibly heavy, its contents holding the truth she and Marcus had fought so hard to uncover. She stared at it for a long moment, her breath uneven. The faint echoes of the explosion that consumed the Order's headquarters lingered in her mind, a stark reminder of Marcus's sacrifice.

"Marcus," she whispered, her voice cracking. "You didn't die for nothing."

Her legs trembled as she pushed herself forward, finding a nearby bench to sit on. She pulled out her laptop, her hands shaking as she plugged in the drive. The files opened instantly, revealing the trove of data they had extracted—the Order's plans, their network, the detailed steps of "The Convergence."

Eliza's fingers hovered over the keyboard before typing quickly, transferring the files to secure servers. She uploaded everything to trusted media outlets, whistleblower platforms, and independent investigators. With every file sent, she felt the weight on her chest lift slightly.

Her phone buzzed with incoming messages—journalists, activists, and anonymous contacts reacting to the data dump.

"This is explosive. Where did this come from?" one journalist asked.

"We've been chasing rumors of this for years," an investigator wrote. *"This changes everything."*

Eliza responded sparingly, her focus narrowing as she sent the final files. She leaned back against the bench, her heart racing. It wasn't over—not yet—but the first step had been taken.

Her phone buzzed again, this time with an anonymous number. She hesitated before answering, her voice steady despite the exhaustion. "Who is this?"

A familiar voice came through the line, cold and deliberate. "You think this will stop us, Eliza?"

Her grip tightened on the phone. "It's a start."

The voice chuckled darkly. "The Order is more than you can imagine. You've only scratched the surface."

"And you've underestimated me," she shot back. "This isn't the end. It's the beginning."

The line went dead, and Eliza lowered the phone slowly. The conversation left a bitter taste in her mouth, but it also ignited something deeper—a fire that wouldn't be extinguished. She stood, slipping the phone into her pocket as the first rays of sunlight illuminated the empty street.

Behind her, the city began to stir, oblivious to the war waged beneath its surface. Eliza walked forward, her steps steady despite the pain. Her thoughts were on Marcus, on her mother, and on the countless lives the Order had manipulated.

A voice cut through her reverie, soft but resolute. "You did it," she imagined Marcus saying, his smirk vivid in her memory.

"No," she murmured to herself, her gaze fixed on the horizon. "Not yet. But I will."

The final scene showed her entering a nondescript building, her laptop tucked under her arm. She sat at a desk cluttered with papers and maps, each one marked with new targets, new leads. On the wall, a large board displayed the names of key Order members, many of them crossed out but others still glaring in red ink.

The camera lingered on her face, her expression a mix of grief and determination. Her final words echoed in the empty room, a vow that carried the weight of everything she had lost and everything she still had to fight for.

"This isn't over," she said softly. "Not until they're gone."

The scene faded, but the sound of the city grew louder—an ever-present reminder that while the fight was far from over, cracks were beginning to form in the Order's façade. And Eliza Kain was ready to exploit every one of them.

Epilogue
The Shadows Endure

The city skyline gleamed in the early dawn, a thin haze of golden light breaking through the smog. Eliza stood on the edge of a rooftop, the chill of the morning wind cutting through her jacket. She clutched her mother's journal tightly, its leather cover worn and scuffed. The weight of its contents—and the truths it had helped her uncover—felt heavier than ever. Below her, the city churned with life, oblivious to the battle she had fought in its depths. The Concordant Order's secrets had been laid bare, their influence chipped away piece by piece, but the scars of the struggle remained. Marcus's absence was a void she couldn't fill, a constant ache that sat like a stone in her chest.

The memory of his final moments haunted her, the way he'd stood firm in the face of certain death so she could escape with the evidence. His sacrifice wasn't just a loss; it was a call to action, a reminder of what was at stake. Eliza's phone buzzed in her pocket, jolting her from her thoughts. She pulled it out, her fingers brushing the cracked screen. A message blinked up at her: *"Your work isn't done. The Order still moves in the shadows. Be ready."* She exhaled sharply, her grip tightening on the device. The message came from the same anonymous source that had tipped her off to the Order's headquarters—a source she still didn't fully trust. But they'd been right before, and that was enough to keep her listening.

Back in her small, cluttered apartment, Eliza sat at her desk, the journal spread open in front of her alongside maps and files. She had shared the evidence with journalists and investigators she trusted, people who could carry the torch in ways she couldn't. The stories had started to break, the media swirling with whispers of a secretive organization and the conspiracy it had orchestrated beneath the city. But the cracks in the Order's façade didn't mean it had crumbled. Eliza knew better than to assume victory. The Order's reach was vast, its roots deep. What she had exposed was just the beginning—a prelude to a larger battle.

Her laptop chimed, pulling her attention to the screen. An encrypted file had appeared in her inbox, its sender untraceable. She clicked it open cautiously, her heart pounding as the contents loaded. Blueprints for another city, another set of tunnels marked with the same symbols she had spent months deciphering. Her breath caught. The Order wasn't just confined to her city—it was global. She leaned back in her chair, her mind racing. If the Concordant Order had this kind of reach, then dismantling it would require more than she could do alone. But she wouldn't stop. Marcus's voice echoed in her mind, teasing and sharp: *"You're stubborn as hell, Kain."*

"Yes, I am," she whispered to the empty room. The city's rhythms carried on as the weeks passed, the fallout from her revelations rippling through political and corporate spheres. High-profile resignations, sudden bankruptcies, and whispered scandals painted a picture of power structures shaken but not shattered. Eliza watched it all from the sidelines, her role in the chaos carefully hidden.

Late one night, as the city settled into uneasy silence, Eliza found herself back in the tunnels. She retraced her steps to where Marcus had made his stand, the air heavy with memories. The rubble had been cleared, the scars of their battle erased, but she could still feel his presence. "You deserved more than this," she murmured, her voice barely audible in the darkness. "But I'll make it mean something. I promise."

A faint noise behind her made her spin, her hand instinctively reaching for the taser at her hip. A shadow detached itself from the wall, stepping into the dim light. It was a woman, her features obscured by a hood. "Eliza Kain," the woman said, her voice low but steady. "You've stirred the hornet's nest." Eliza didn't lower her guard. "Who are you?"

"A friend," the woman replied. "Or an enemy, depending on your next move." "Cryptic much?" Eliza shot back, her eyes narrowing. The woman chuckled, the sound devoid of humor. "The Concordant Order isn't done with you. But if you're smart, you'll leave this city. Their reach extends far, and your fight here is only one piece of a much larger puzzle."

Eliza frowned, her grip on her weapon tightening. "Why should I trust you?" "You shouldn't," the woman admitted. "But you don't have many allies left, do you?" Eliza considered her words carefully, the weight of the journal in her bag grounding her. "If you have information, share it. Otherwise, get out of my way." The woman nodded, tossing a small flash drive onto the ground. "This will show you where to look next. But be careful, Kain. The deeper you dig, the more dangerous it gets."

Before Eliza could respond, the woman disappeared into the shadows, leaving her alone with the drive. She picked it up, her pulse pounding as she slipped it into her pocket. Whatever was on it, she knew it would lead to more questions than answers. In the days that followed, Eliza began to piece together the threads of a global conspiracy, her focus shifting beyond the confines of her city. She worked in secrecy, her every move calculated, her trust hard-won and sparingly given. The fight against the Order was far from over, but she welcomed the challenge.

One night, as she stared at her mother's journal, a memory surfaced—her mother's voice, calm and resolute: *"The truth is never easy, Eliza, but it's always worth fighting for."* Eliza closed the journal, her resolve hardening. The Order had underestimated her once. They wouldn't make that mistake again.

With the city at her back and the world ahead of her, Eliza Kain stepped into the unknown, her fight far from finished but her purpose clearer than ever. The shadows endured, but so did she—and she was ready to bring the light.

Milton Keynes UK
Ingram Content Group UK Ltd.
UKHW042036031224
452078UK00001B/193